"Only a month until the trial, Julia." Gavin tried to sound encouraging.

"Don't you think I know that?" Her voice had a hard edge to it, though her eyes were rimmed with tears.

Again, he had to remind himself that this anger was not about him. This was about her seven years of confinement and abuse.

"I know you've been through a lot."

She turned to face him, shaking her head. "You have no idea. Seven years of living in that house with all the locks on the doors..."

He didn't react to her anger. If she needed to vent, that was fine with him.

Gavin reached toward her. She stepped back, exhausted and shivering, tears streaming down her face. Without a word, he picked up the coat and draped it over her shoulders. She fell against his chest weeping.

Slowly, tentatively, he wrapped his arms around her and held her while she cried. Her soft hair brushed the bottom of his chin. The air around them grew cold.

He held her until she stopped crying.

Books by Sharon Dunn

Love Inspired Suspense

Dead Ringer
Night Prey
Her Guardian

SHARON DUNN

has always loved writing, but didn't decide to write for publication until she was expecting her first baby. Pregnancy makes you do crazy things. Three kids, many articles and two mystery series later, she still hasn't found her sanity. Her books have won awards, including a Book of the Year award from American Christian Fiction Writers. She was also a finalist for an *RT Book Reviews* Inspirational Book of the Year award.

Sharon has performed in theater and church productions, gotten degrees in film production and history and worked for many years as a college tutor and instructor. Despite the fact that her résumé looks as if she couldn't decide what she wanted to be when she grew up, all the education and experience have played a part in helping her write good stories.

When she isn't writing or taking her kids to activities, she reads, plays board games and contemplates organizing her closet. In addition to her three kids, Sharon lives with her husband of twenty-two years, three cats and lots of dust bunnies.

Her
Guardian

SHARON DUNN

Love Inspired

Recycling programs
for this product may
not exist in your area.

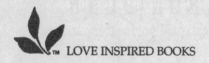

™ LOVE INSPIRED BOOKS

ISBN-13: 978-0-373-44449-6

HER GUARDIAN

www.LoveInspiredBooks.com

Printed in U.S.A.

I will repay you for the years the locusts have eaten.
—*Joel* 2:25

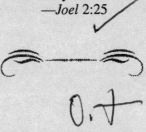

For my husband, Michael,
who loves me unconditionally.

ONE

Professional bodyguard Gavin Shane glanced around the small department store as a sense of foreboding spread through him. He looked at the young woman he had been hired to protect. His client, Julia Randel, picked up a bottle of tester perfume and sprayed it onto her thin wrist. A smile graced her pretty face. She didn't seem alarmed.

The other shoppers whirled benignly through the store. Yet everything in Gavin's training told him it had been a mistake to stop here, to let Julia out in public. Mentally he kicked himself for his poor judgment. He should have said no when she had looked at him with large blue eyes and asked to stop on their way to the secure location. Her request had held a tone of desperation, as if stopping to shop at this tiny department store meant the world to her.

Julia showed him the perfume bottle, her expression bright. "I think I would like to get this one."

Gavin stepped toward her. The citrus scent of the perfume she had just sprayed hung in the air. As he scanned the faces of the other customers, he couldn't pinpoint his reason for unease…something just felt off. If he had learned nothing else in his ten years as a bodyguard, it was to trust his instincts.

He leaned close and whispered, "We need to go."

"What?" She shook her head as the exuberance he'd seen a moment before disappeared. She turned a half circle, studying the people around her, disbelief clouding her features. "No, it can't be."

Julia was coping with the threat she was under through denial. He'd seen it before. She was shutting down. He had to push her past it. "Put the perfume back. Let's get out of here."

"Elijah's followers couldn't have found me that easily." She looked up at him, her eyes pleading. "They couldn't have." Her voice faltered.

"I don't think we should take chances." He didn't want to feed into the constant anxiety she must be under, but to be on the safe side, they had to leave immediately.

One of the customers caught Gavin's attention. A man dressed in a dated suit circled closer to Julia through the cosmetic section. How peculiar. Men usually didn't shop for lipstick and mascara. Gavin maintained a surface calm, but adrenaline charged through his muscles as he prepared to grab Julia and run.

Go, now, go.

Julia had been held captive for seven years by the cult leader Elijah True. Now two years after her escape, she was ready to testify against him. That meant his followers had ramped up their efforts to make sure she didn't set foot in a courtroom.

"Put the perfume back." Struggling to keep the sense of urgency out of his voice, he gripped her arm above the elbow.

"All right, if that's what we have to do." A tone of

despair colored her words. She set the perfume on the display shelf. Her hand brushed over the top of the bottle. "I wish I had time to get this."

Why was she so fixated on getting such a small thing as perfume?

The man in the suit moved down the aisle toward them. He didn't have that vagueness in the eyes or long hair and beard that was common to male cult members, but the way he narrowed his eyes at Julia made alarm bells go off in Gavin's head.

"We gotta move, now." As gently as he could, he hooked his arm through hers and pulled her toward the door. She allowed herself to be directed out to the street. The winter cold of February in Montana hit them as he pulled his keys from his pocket. Julia rubbed her bare arms. She'd left her coat in the SUV.

He could be totally wrong about the threat, but it wasn't a chance he was willing to take. He looked directly into her blue eyes, hoping to shake her from her inertia. "Please trust me when I say we have to go."

The man in the suit came out on the sidewalk. Julia pulled free of Gavin's arm and stared blankly at him.

The denial was paralyzing her. He had to break her free of it. "Your father hired me to protect you. Do what I say. Get in the car." He enunciated each word.

Her lips drew into a tight, hard line. She shook her head, but she complied. As he slipped behind the wheel of the SUV, he checked his rearview mirror. The man in the suit was talking on his cell phone and casting furtive glances in their direction. It was possible he was only phoning a friend. All the same, Gavin was reminded of the mantra his boss down in Florida had repeated over and over. *It was always better to be paranoid than dead.*

Gavin pulled away from the curb and sped up as soon as he reached the city limits.

"When I say we need to go, we need to go." He shifted into fourth gear and revved the engine. He took in a deep breath. Being upset with her wouldn't do either of them any good.

Julia stared straight ahead. "It would have only taken a minute to get that perfume."

Why was she bringing up the perfume again? There was something deeper going on here. "It was a minute we didn't have," he said.

Frustration rose up in her voice. "Are you sure they were there? I didn't see anybody."

She still didn't want to believe that they were after her again. "Your father told me that you might not recognize all the cult members." He checked the rearview mirror. "A lot of them don't live at the compound anymore. They've fanned out into the surrounding towns, but they are still loyal to Elijah." A dark blue van had eased in behind them. When Gavin let up on the accelerator, the van remained behind them instead of passing.

"That's true." She combed her fingers through her long, blond hair. "I didn't even get to know many of the cult members at the compound." Her voice was a harsh whisper filled with pain. "Elijah mostly kept me in his house." She shook her head. "How did they find us so easily?"

"I don't know." If it had just been the man in the suit, he would have dismissed the incident as him being overly cautious. But the van was clearly tailing them, which meant his instincts had been right. "They must have been watching your father's house for days waiting for us to leave. That's the only way they could have found us."

Elijah's followers had been a concern since his arrest, but they had done nothing overt enough for the police to justify spending tight funds on protection. Though he could not prove a clear connection to Elijah, Julia's father had become alarmed when strange cars were parked outside their house, and it had looked as though someone might be going through their garbage. With the trial less than a month away, William Randel had hired Gavin and decided to move his daughter to a safe and unknown location.

Now as he watched the van edge closer, Gavin realized that all of William Randel's suspicions were confirmed.

In his peripheral vision, he could see that Julia's cheeks had turned crimson. She was growing more agitated as the reality of her situation sank in.

"What's going on?" He spoke as gently as he could manage.

"It's like that monster still has me in a prison even though I got away from him. I did what Elijah ordered me to do for seven years. Then I did what my father and the counselor said for two years. Now I have to listen to you." Her voice broke. "I just feel…like I'll never be free…that's all."

Gavin's glance bounced from the road and back to Julia. Sympathy washed through him as he comprehended why she was so upset. He'd known her for less than a week, and their conversations at the house had been brief. All the abuse and loss she had been through made any words of comfort he could come up with sound trite.

She laced her hands together. "Sorry, I know this is

the way it has to be. I'm…it's just hard sometimes. Nine years is a long time."

The van was nearly touching his bumper. They'd have to talk later. He pressed the accelerator. "I've got to lose these guys."

Julia craned her neck and then turned back around, sinking in her seat. "That's them, isn't it?" A tinge of fear colored her words.

"I thought we took enough precautions." He kept his voice neutral, not wanting to add fuel to the panic she must be feeling. This wasn't her doing, it was his. They never should have gone into that store. Gavin pressed the accelerator. The car hugged the curves as the needle pressed past one hundred. The SUV didn't handle like a race car, but it would do.

Julia gripped the door. "Do you always go this fast?"

"Only when I'm trying to lose someone." The distance between the van and the SUV increased. "Let's just get you to that safe house your father set up."

"If we don't crash first, right?"

"Julia, would you trust me? I've done this before." Maintaining the same high speed, he drove for a few more miles. No sign of the van. He hit the blinker and veered toward an exit ramp.

She sat up straighter. "This isn't the way we need to go."

He came to a small town and zigzagged through the streets. "I can't take you directly to the secure location until we are sure we're not being followed." If the van could tail them through all this, he'd be impressed.

She pushed her head against the back of the seat. He could sense her rising frustration in the car's confined space. "I understand," she said softly, as though she was resigned to the conditions she had to live with.

"We'll just drive around for a while." He injected a false cheerfulness into his voice as he pulled back out on to a two-lane road. "These back roads can be kind of nice to look at."

She turned her head away from him. He drove without talking for an hour. He had to remind himself that her frustration wasn't because of something he had done, though he was the target. Even before he had been hired by William Randel, he'd known who Julia was. Two years ago, her face was splashed across the tabloids. Julia had been abducted at thirteen by Elijah True. Elijah had been born Leonard Reef but had changed his name, called himself a prophet and founded what he called the True Church.

Seven years later, after witnessing Elijah murder another cult member, Julia had slipped away from the cluster of houses that had been built in the remote Badlands of Montana. He'd seen the news photos of the compound—rows of trailers and modular homes surrounded by barbed wire. In an effort to ease their dependence on the outside world, the cult members grew much of their own food and kept goats and sheep.

Gavin suspected that the lawyers had had something to do with the lack of details about the murder charges against Elijah in the news stories. Most of the coverage had focused on Julia's captivity and escape. She had run five miles in winter conditions to a small town to get help. It had taken two years to put together the murder and kidnapping charges. Only Elijah and one other follower had been aware of the kidnapping. Elijah had told the other cult members that Julia was a niece he'd received custody of.

Even though they had not been a part of the kidnapping, the forty or so families at the compound viewed Julia as the enemy who had betrayed their innocent leader.

The True Church, which borrowed bits and pieces of theology from almost every other religion, seemed to be based around a distrust of the government. Their hypocrisy showed though, in that they had no problem collecting welfare checks. A belief that they were special and all outsiders were woefully misled also came out in the interviews that had been done with ex-cult members.

The words of Julia's father as he briefed Gavin floated back into his memory. "My daughter has had two years of counseling and she is doing much better, but she is still…fragile. We initially thought we would hire a much older man, but your experience is quite impressive for someone so young. I trust you won't think Julia is romantic material."

Though it seemed an odd request, William's protectiveness of his daughter was understandable; Gavin had given his word. After William Randel's description of his daughter, Gavin had expected a shrinking violet. The woman with the white-blond hair falling past her shoulders and intense blue eyes had exuded poise and strength as she reached out to shake Gavin's hand the first time he met her. The newspaper pictures hadn't done her justice. She was a stunning woman.

So far, he had seen none of the fragility William had referenced. Anyone who could run that far in freezing conditions, avoiding capture, had to be strong and smart. He admired that.

Still, he needed a level of cooperation from her if he was to do his job. He tried to understand her point of view. She was tired of confinement, tired of taking orders. He got that. She'd come this far; it was only a month until the trial now. With the end in sight, maybe all the emotion she had pushed down was rising to the surface.

Gavin focused on his driving. Ice covering the trees that lined the two-lane highway made them look as if they were made of crystal. At least the roads were clear. He checked his mirrors one more time. Nobody behind them. No cars had passed them in the last thirty minutes.

"We can stop if you like," he said.

Julia turned back toward him. "I don't need to stop."

"I just thought maybe you would like to get some fresh air." He infused his voice with as much pleasantness as he could muster. They didn't have to be best friends, but he needed her to trust his judgment. They had gotten lucky with this incident. Next time, her hesitation could cost her her life. "It's only a month until the trial, Julia."

He caught a flash of hurt in her expression before she jerked in her seat and bent her head allowing her hair to fall over her face.

He pulled over on a shoulder of the road and killed the engine. They sat in silence for a long moment. Finally, he pushed his door open. "You can stay here if you want. I'm going to stretch my legs."

He got out of the car and walked a few feet away. In the distance, two horses gamboled through a snowy field. The sky was a robin's-egg blue. He'd missed winter. Florida had been nice, but five years away from Montana was too long. When he exhaled, his breath was visible. Behind him, the car door opened and slammed.

He turned to face Julia. She crossed her arms over her body.

"You have a coat in the car." He walked to the back of his car and retrieved a pink ski jacket. He draped it over her shoulders. She didn't put her arms through the sleeves. "It's a nice coat."

The raw anguish on her face shot daggers through him. "My father had a female friend buy it for me. I can't go out shopping for myself—too much media and always the fear that Elijah's followers will be around." She angled her head away from him and hunched over.

Now he understood why the perfume had meant so much to her. It would have been something she had picked out and bought herself. She just wanted the normal experience of going into a store and purchasing something. She really had been a prisoner in her father's house. "There will come a time when you can choose your own coat."

She stared at the ground. "I don't even like pink. Blue is my favorite color."

"Only a month, Julia." He tried to sound encouraging.

She lifted her head and looked straight at him. "Don't you think I know how many days until the trial?" Her voice had a hard edge to it, though her eyes were rimmed with tears.

Again, he had to remind himself that this anger was not about him, though it was directed at him. This was about her seven years of confinement and abuse. This was about the injustice that had been done to her.

She whirled away from him. The coat fell to the

ground. He picked it up and placed it over her shoulders again. "I know you've been through a lot."

She turned to face him, shaking her head. "You have no idea."

His heart swelled with sympathy. "I wasn't meaning to minimize—"

Even with the veneer of anger, he could see the pain behind her eyes.

He reached out to put a supportive hand on her shoulder. "I know that—"

She pushed his hand away. "Seven years of living in that house with all the locks on the doors...of listening to his twisted logic."

He didn't react to her anger. If she needed to vent, that was fine with him. Anything to let her know that he was on her side.

"Seven years of never going into town, of barely getting to talk to people except for Marlena." Something visibly broke inside Julia when she said the murdered woman's name. She kicked the ground and crossed her arms over her body.

He reached toward her. She stepped back, exhausted and shivering, tears streaming down her face. Without a word, he picked up the coat and draped it over her shoulders. She fell against his chest weeping.

Slowly, tentatively, he wrapped his arms around her and held her while she cried. Her soft hair brushed the bottom of his chin. The air around them grew cold. He held her until she stopped crying and pulled back.

"I didn't mean to lose it like that." She swiped at her eyes. "I'm sorry I got your shirt wet."

He shook his head. "Doesn't matter." The look of embarrassment on her face tugged at his heart. She had nothing to be ashamed of. "Are you ready to get going?"

She nodded and trudged back to the SUV. After she opened the door, she looked up at him with an expression that suggested they'd made some headway in the trust department.

He only hoped the rest of the day would go more smoothly than it had started.

TWO

Julia settled into the passenger seat just as Gavin opened the door and placed the key in the ignition. Her cheeks still felt hot. She hadn't meant to lose control. The past seven years, with Elijah calling the shots, had been about maintaining control. Whatever absurd proclamation came out of his mouth, she had simply pretended to agree to it. She knew her Bible well enough to know that he was distorting Scripture to justify his actions, but she had never argued with him.

Elijah True had done landscaping work for Julia's father. Two months later, he had come back and snatched her when she was walking to her piano lesson. For seven years, the police had never connected him to the kidnapping.

Despite Elijah's need to control everything and everyone, Marlena had some kind of sway over him as long as she remained the doting wife in public. Marlena had been unable to have children. Elijah had kidnapped Julia when Marlena had threatened to leave, saying that Julia could be the child she always wanted.

She had protected Julia from being married off to the man of Elijah's choosing. Until the night Elijah had grown impatient, demanding it was time that Julia be married. Elijah had locked Julia in her room, but she had heard all of the fight that led to Marlena's death.

Julia had thought about escape a thousand times before, had even tried a couple of times only to have Elijah increase her confinement. It wasn't until that night when Marlena died…that courage and the opportunity for escape had come together. In the chaos that followed Marlena's death, Elijah had forgotten to lock the outside doors, and she had been able to jimmy the lock to her room…she hadn't gotten out fast enough to save Marlena, though. With Elijah out of the house, she had rushed to see that Marlena wasn't breathing and knew that she had to get out.

The last thing she heard as she crawled through the barbed wire that surrounded the houses was Elijah gathering his followers in the dirt street telling a distorted story of how Julia had pushed Marlena and caused her to hit her head, attempting to stir up the others enough to harm Julia. For most of her run through the dark and cold, she had cried for Marlena.

Gavin's gentle voice brought her back to reality. He shoved the key in the ignition. "Do you want the heater on?"

"Just a little bit. We'll be sweating if you turn it on high." The two years of counseling had been good, the nightmares no longer plagued her, the anxiety was under control. Her counselor had told her that the next stage in her recovery would be anger. She hadn't been prepared for the strength of it. Poor Gavin had had to witness it.

When her father had told her he'd hired a bodyguard, Gavin Shane was not what she had expected. He was tall and muscular as a bodyguard should be, but there was none of the cold brusqueness she had counted on.

Gavin's light brown hair with blond sun-streaks and the sunglasses he always wore made him look more like a surfer than a bodyguard. The rich brown of his skin only added to the effect.

"Marlena was the woman who died, right?" He spoke slowly, choosing his words carefully. He was probably afraid of another outburst from her.

"Yes, she was Elijah's common-law wife. She was only five years older than me...but she was kind to me, like a mom would be." Marlena had confessed to Julia that even though she always threatened to leave to keep Elijah under control, she really had no place to go. Besides, she had told Julia, Elijah treated her way better than the family she had come from.

Despite all the abuse she had suffered in her own family and the psychological badgering with Elijah, there had been a deeper goodness to Marlena. She could have been mean to Julia or jealous of Elijah's leering glances. Instead, she had wanted to protect Julia from all that she had been through. "She could be a little rough around the edges, but she was a good person. She was the biggest reason I am not more messed up because of what happened." Her hand fluttered to her throat as pain stabbed at her heart.

After checking for oncoming cars, he pulled out on to the road. "If you don't want to talk about it..."

And she thought she had hidden her sadness. He seemed to be pretty good at picking up on her feelings. She didn't know if she liked that about him or not. "I'm fine."

Maybe it was just out of habit, but she felt her emotional shields going up. Feelings were something she learned to keep to herself in the cult.

"So you know the woman who runs the hot springs spa where I'm taking you?"

She was grateful he had switched to a safer subject. "No, the police advised my father to find someone who couldn't be linked to us in any way. Elizabeth Johnson was a friend of my mother's from high school. She got in touch with my dad when she read about the upcoming trial and offered her place."

Gavin tapped his thumbs on the steering wheel. "I'm going to have to stop for gas at the next town. This detour cost us some fuel. I don't want to run out before we get to the hot springs."

"The last sign said there was a town coming up in six miles." She could make small talk, too. Maybe that would be the safest thing to do. "So Dad said you moved back up here from Florida?"

"Yeah, I was born and raised in Montana."

"What made you decide to come back?"

His cheek twitched and, as though a curtain were falling over his face, his features hardened. "It was just time."

Julia sat back in her seat. For some reason, he didn't want to talk about Florida. She'd touched a nerve even with her small talk.

The silence caused a familiar sadness to surface. Pain jabbed at her insides. Before her life had been turned upside down, she had had dreams. She was going to go to college and study fashion design or dentistry. Someday she would fall in love, marry and have kids. Just simple ordinary dreams…and they had been taken from her.

Though it was hard, she could not focus on what she had lost. The Bible verse about God restoring the years the locusts had eaten gave her hope. She would get her life back. Sometimes, though, all this continued confinement made her doubt that day would ever come.

Gavin hit his blinker and took the next exit. The town consisted of a truck stop and a block or two of shops and a hotel. After parking by a pump, Gavin got out of the car.

Julia stared at Gavin as he walked past the windshield. He never stopped looking around, constantly assessing his surroundings. Old fears returned. The last time they had stopped, things hadn't gone well. She shouldn't have insisted on stopping at that store. A false sense of freedom had overtaken her as they'd sailed down the road.

She didn't want to be alone with her fear in this car. Being close to him made her feel safer. She pushed the door open and circled around to the gas pumps where Gavin was standing. "Can you show me how to put gas in a car?"

Gavin straightened slightly. Though she caught just a flash of it, he did a good job of hiding his shock. "You don't know how?"

She fought past the embarrassment that rose up over all these simple things that she didn't know how to do. She wouldn't learn if she didn't ask. "My father took me out sometimes at night to practice driving when the media wasn't likely to be around. We never got around to the gas lesson."

Warmth came into Gavin's eyes. His voice softened. "Sure, I can show you."

He walked her through twisting the gas cap, zeroing out the pump and placing the nozzle in the gas tank. She relished this moment, just standing with the brisk air buffeting her, doing something that most people took for granted.

He glanced toward the store that was part of the truck stop. "Are you hungry?"

"Can I go with you and pick out my own snack?" She was almost afraid to ask the question. After what had happened at the department store, would he tell her to stay in the car?

"I have to go in to pay for the gas, anyway. I don't want to leave you out here alone." He touched her lightly on the shoulder. "Stay close to me."

Julia nodded and made her way to the store. She could feel Gavin's body heat as he walked behind her. She'd just have to get used to the claustrophobic feeling that went with the close proximity of another person. She didn't like it, but she would have to get used to it. She understood the need for a bodyguard. She wanted Elijah put away for good, but a part of her longed to hop on a plane or bus and run and be free. The long fight against the injustice that had been done to her had left her battle weary. Sometimes the longing for escape into normalcy was so intense.

Once inside the store, Julia gazed up and down the aisle. In addition to the food items, she noticed hats and T-shirts. She passed an aisle that contained makeup, aspirin and other things a drug store would carry. This store must function as the everything store for the small town.

She contemplated some packaged donuts. Her awareness of her surroundings heightened when Gavin pivoted suddenly and stalked toward the window.

He turned back to her, squaring his broad shoulders.

His vigilant soldier stance made her heart beat faster.

"What is it?" Her voice was hoarse. She swallowed to quell the rising fear.

He pointed to the front of the store. "We got company."

THREE

Gavin leaned close and shout-whispered, "To the back of the store. Now—go."

Julia didn't move. One look at the wide, round eyes told him she was frozen by panic. He pressed on her lower back, steering her to a rack of hats and T-shirts.

A thought occurred to him. He grabbed one of the hats off the display. "Blue is your favorite color, right?"

She nodded.

He slipped the hat over her head. "Tuck your hair in and stay at the back of the store until I get a read on what's happening with them. That blond hair is too easy to identify at a distance."

Gavin stalked down the aisle grabbing hair dye and the donuts Julia had been eyeballing earlier. He set the items on the counter in front of the clerk and then pointed to where Julia stood. "My girlfriend would like that hat, too."

While the clerk rang up the purchases, Gavin watched the dark blue van that had just pulled up outside. The last time they had seen the van it had been in a rearview mirror, but he was pretty sure it was the same vehicle.

Two men, both with long hair and beards, got out. They hesitated in front of his SUV, studied it for a moment.

Good thing Julia had gone with him into the store, or the bearded men might be pulling her out of the SUV right now.

"There you go, sir." The clerk handed him a bag.

The two men made a beeline for the store.

When he looked over to where the hats were, Julia had vanished. His heart hammered in his chest as he took large strides across the store. She wasn't behind the display rack, either. Shaking off the rising panic he glanced from one corner of the store to the next, then walked the aisles.

Gavin ducked his head behind a rack of greeting cards when the two men came inside. They feigned interest in the soft drinks at the front of the store while they continued to study the room. One of them had a distinctive bulge on his side that indicated a gun.

Only two other customers walked the aisles, an older man and a teenage girl. Gavin wandered toward the snack shelves, searching without turning his head too much, keeping his back to the two men. Julia must have gone into the restroom. He bolted across the floor and stepped into the narrow hallway between restrooms and the "Employees Only" door. He took note of a back door exit he had passed as he gently rapped on the restroom door designated for women. "Julia," he whispered.

She opened the door a crack. "I knew by the look on your face I had to hide." Her voice was steady. She'd overcome the initial panic and pulled herself together. She showed remarkable composure, considering.

He directed her out into the tiny hallway between bathrooms and then pointed toward the back door. They would only be exposed for a few seconds, and her blond hair stuffed under the cap no longer functioned as a beacon.

"Walk slowly...don't call attention to yourself."

Again she froze, fear written on her face. She'd spotted the two men. Her pulse beat visibly at the side of her neck. Was she going to give in to the fear after all?

Urgency pressed on him from all sides. "We. Have. To. Go," he whispered, emphasizing every word.

She focused on him and squared her shoulders. "Let's move."

Gavin ushered Julia out of the hallway and slipped in behind her, shielding her from view. Each footstep was a drum beat. Slowly. No one will notice. The door was five feet away.

The bell on the front door dinged and two loud children, followed by a mother and father, stepped in. The noise of the children drew everyone's attention.

Julia yanked open the door. Gavin almost fell on top of her as they slipped outside. "Now we can run." He grabbed her hand, pulling her along the side of the building toward the car. Adrenaline surged through him.

His feet slid over a patch of ice. He recovered, but Julia stumbled. She let out a cry.

"Are you okay?"

"I scraped my leg against something." She indicated her torn jeans. A jagged piece of scrap metal was frozen in the ice, sharp end pointing up and glistening with Julia's blood. "I'm okay. We can deal with it later."

With Julia favoring her right leg, they ran. Gavin wrapped his arms around her waist and helped her to the car. As he started the engine, he glanced at the windows of the store. No sign of the bearded men. They must have worked their way toward the back, but it would only take minutes before they noticed the SUV was gone.

His heart thudded as he pulled out on to the road. He clicked on his GPS. All these detours had probably turned a five-hour drive into a ten-hour one. He couldn't go to the secure house until he was sure they weren't being followed.

Out of breath, Julia rested her head against the back of the seat. Her palm was pressed to her chest. "My heart is racing."

"You handled yourself just fine." It was a huge step in their being able to work together that she had muscled through the initial fear and panic and made smart choices.

He drove through the two blocks of downtown, glancing at the GPS. How long were they going to have to play cat and mouse? He picked a route that would take them in a wide arc before they got to the location her father had set up. The route showed two small towns before they arrived at the hot springs.

Julia opened the bag and pulled out the donuts. "Thank you." She lifted the box of hair dye out. "For me?"

"As much as I like that hat…" The floppy ears on the blue knitted cap made her look kind of cute. "I think we need a more permanent solution to you being so easy to spot from a distance."

Julia studied the box. "Sunset red."

He adjusted his sunglasses on top of his head. "I wasn't looking at colors. I just grabbed one."

"Red hair might be okay." Her voice fell half an octave. "One of the reasons Elijah took me was the blond hair. He said it made me look like an angel."

He drove for a few more minutes. She winced and exhaled heavily.

"What is it?"

Her back arched in pain. "My leg. I think the cut is worse than I thought." She gripped the arm rest.

"Can you hold on for just a bit?" He checked the rearview mirror. No sign of the van, but it was still too soon to stop. "I'll get us to a place where I can take care of that."

Her lips were drawn into a tight line. "Okay."

He had to take her mind off the pain. "That was some fast thinking, slipping into the bathroom." He had been impressed with how she had strategized. They might make a good team after all. Gavin increased his speed as the countryside opened up in front of them.

"I have a few good ideas." A tiny gasp escaped her lips. Her hand curled into a fist.

He responded with a sympathetic shudder. She was really hurting. "Just hang on." He checked his mirrors. No one was following them on the rural road. Hopefully, the van had pulled out on to the highway.

Her stiff posture indicated she was still in pain.

He drove for twenty minutes more until he found a shoulder to pull off on. "Stay where you are." He grabbed a first-aid kit from under the backseat and hustled to her side of the car.

When he opened the door, she was pale. Her jeans had a huge blood-soaked patch. He pulled his pocket-knife out of his coat. "I'll just cut the fabric away."

She nodded, breathing in air through gritted teeth.

The gash was short but deep. She jerked when he placed the disinfectant on it. He pulled a strand of gauze from the kit and wrapped it around her calf. "Better?"

She offered him a half nod. Obviously, she was still in pain.

He dug through the kit until he found ibuprofen and grabbed his water bottle. "For the pain." He cupped her hand in his and placed the tablet in her palm. The back of her hand was smooth like silk.

He lifted his head and looked into her blue eyes. He saw strength, an indomitable spirit. "That should help ease your pain." He was struck by the paradox of her life. Here was a woman who had been through more than most people would ever face. She could certainly deal with more than the average person. Yet she didn't know how to put gas in a car.

Her lip quivered. Sympathy rushed through him. He reached up and brushed his knuckles over her cheek. "That leg is going to be okay."

Julia drew strength from the intensity of Gavin's gaze. The warmth of his touch on her cheek still lingered when he pulled away. Carefully, gently, he lifted her leg and helped her to face forward in the car. She tensed when a fresh dagger of pain sliced up her calf. That ibuprofen couldn't kick in soon enough.

Gavin's expression communicated empathy. "Ready to go?"

She nodded. "I'll be okay. Let's just get to the hot springs."

Gavin drove down the country road. The throbbing in her leg subsided. Julia shared her donuts. The sky turned from blue to gray while they made small talk about what they passed on the road, often falling into silence. The setting sun created a display of orange and purple on the horizon.

Their endless zigzagging to shake off the pursuers

had cost them a lot of time. Gavin pulled back on to the main highway. It was dark by the time the headlights illuminated a sign that indicated the exit for Silver Cliff, the town that was close to the hot springs.

"Can you read me the directions your father wrote down?"

He handed her a folded note he had stuffed into the cup holder. His fingers brushed over hers. A spark of energy surged up her arm. The sudden warmth that spread through her surprised her.

She took the note and unfolded it, bringing it closer to her eyes to decipher her father's spidery scrawl. "My father should have been a doctor, not a lit professor." She read the directions.

As Gavin repeated the directions back to her, she shook off the unexpected heat of attraction. At a time when most girls just started to think boys didn't have cooties, her life had become a nightmare. After her escape, male friends she had known from when she was thirteen had come to the house to visit. Their company had helped break the monotony of confinement, but her awkwardness in conversation with men was a reminder of how a whole chunk of her life had been ripped away. She had never felt anything more than friendship toward any of the young men who had come over.

Julia wasn't quite sure what to think about the surge of electricity Gavin's touch had caused. Everything was so new. She was twenty-two-years-old and had never even been on a date. She cut her eyes at the man beside her. What would it be like to go on a date with Gavin? The thought made the heat rise to her cheeks, and she was grateful for the darkness that hid her face. She shouldn't be thinking about such things.

The car rolled through the tiny town of Silver Cliff.

They passed the dark windows of a dress shop and a hardware store. At the end of the block, a coffee shop that had a warm glow and a few patrons sitting at tables caught her attention. A young woman hunched over a magazine lifted her head and glanced at Julia. An ache spread through Julia as she placed her hand on the car window. How wonderful would it be to order a coffee and sit and read for an afternoon? She tried to picture herself in the coffee shop doing something so ordinary, something she had never done.

Gavin's soft voice broke through her musing. "Did you say a left turn after Old Goat Road?"

She checked the note again. "Yes, a left turn." She laughed. "That's a funny name, Old Goat Road."

He laughed. "Yeah, I'm sure there's a story behind that. Montana has lots of strange names for places."

"What made you decide to come back to Montana?" His earlier evasiveness to the question had piqued her interest.

"This looks like where we need to go." He turned the car down a dirt road.

Maybe he would answer the question later, or maybe he wanted to keep things professional. He probably hadn't felt the same burst of electricity when their fingers touched. This was just a job to him.

In the dark, she could barely make out the sign that said "Silver Cliff Spa and Hot Springs." One of the chains that held the sign to a post was broken. A hand-painted sign that said "Closed for Renovation" had been nailed to the post. They drove about a mile down the dirt road. The silhouette of several buildings came into view. No light shone in any of the windows.

"I didn't think this place would be so big." Gavin leaned toward the windshield and squinted. "Did your father say exactly where this friend said she would meet us?"

Julia shook her head.

He pulled into a parking lot. Gravel crunched beneath the tires as he drove toward a huge log cabin. "This looks like the main building." He pushed open the car door.

Julia reached back and grabbed her coat before getting out of the car. Her first step on the cut leg sent a pulse of pain through her. Wind rustled the tall cottonwoods that surrounded the building. Creaking branches emanated a sense of loneliness. She shivered.

Favoring the hurt leg, she made her way up the stone path. She scrambled for an explanation as to why the place looked abandoned. "We're getting here a lot later than expected. Maybe she went to sleep. We probably should have called."

"Maybe." Gavin stepped away from the door. He moved a few feet in one direction and then a few feet in the other.

Gratitude for Gavin's vigilance washed through her, and with it guilt over having been difficult. He was so obviously good at his job. Julia wrapped her hand around the doorknob. "The door is not locked." The creaking of the trees in the darkness caused memories to rise to the surface. "Let's go inside. I don't like it out here in the dark."

Gavin hesitated before answering, glancing around one more time. "We are kind of exposed out here anyway." He stood behind Julia as she opened the door, matching his step to hers. "Something doesn't feel right. Stay close to me."

FOUR

Instincts on high alert, Gavin ran his hands along the wall, fumbling for a switch. After he pressed the light on, a warm glow illuminated a huge main room containing leather couches and chairs. A chandelier made out of elk horns hanging from the high ceiling and dark-stained wood dominated the decor.

Julia pointed to the doors on the second floor surrounded by a balcony with a railing made of rough pine. "Those must be the rooms where guests stay."

"Lights are on out there." Glass doors at the far end of the lobby caught Gavin's eye. An outdoor pool with mist rising off it was visible. Gavin called out, "Hello, we're here."

Tension threaded through the silence.

Julia stepped toward a door. "Elizabeth?"

Her inquiry was met with a meow. A large Siamese cat raised her head from the plush chair where she rested. After staring at them for a moment, the cat settled back down to sleep.

Their footsteps echoed on the wood floor as they made their way through the building. Next door to the lobby was a dining hall that had about ten tables. The dining hall led into an industrial-size kitchen that had a separate exit. They stepped outside. A second unlocked building contained indoor hot tubs with white Christmas lights strung from a dome-shaped ceiling that featured skylights. The hot tubs were drained and looked as if they hadn't been used in some time. One of the three doors to the left side of the room was unlabeled. The second had a sign on it that said *library*. The third was a massage room. Still no sign of Elizabeth.

After leaving the hot tub building, Gavin and Julia walked toward a smaller cabin set apart from the other two buildings. In the distance, behind the small cabin, was another building that was probably a barn. Julia limped slightly. Hopefully, the cut would be okay. Their feet crunched in the snow. Gavin ran the events through his head from the time he'd picked Julia up at her father's house. They had been very careful not to leave any kind of a trail that would hint at where they were going.

Though the followers had had no inhibitions about rooting through trash, he doubted they had any high-tech surveillance equipment. The only way they could have found out about this place was to have followed the SUV, and he'd been overly careful to shake the van that had tailed them. It didn't seem probable the followers could have gotten here ahead of them and done something to Elizabeth. Yet he had been surprised at the cult members' ability to locate and follow them in the first place. Maybe they were more sophisticated than he gave them credit for.

Julia gazed into the dark windows of the little cabin. "This must be where she lives. She might have gone to sleep."

Gavin knocked on the door. No response. When he tried the doorknob, it was locked. "I'll call her cell."

From inside the house they heard a cell phone song play. Each bar of music racheted up the tension in the air.

"Looks like wherever she went, she didn't take her phone with her." Julia couldn't hide the worry in her voice.

If there had been a change in plans, why hadn't Elizabeth just called him or at least left a note? He peered into the window, only able to make out the vague outlines of furniture. Most people didn't leave home without their cell phone.

They made their way back to the main building. A half-finished brick wall surrounded the outdoor pool. Bags of cement and a wheelbarrow stood to one side. Julia pushed open the sliding glass doors and stepped back into the lobby. "I'm so hungry my hands are shaking. If I don't eat, I'll get a headache." Anxiety threaded through her voice. "I'm going to see if there's anything to eat in that kitchen."

Gavin hurried to be close to her. He stepped through the dining hall and followed her into the kitchen. Julia had made smart choices at the gas station, but would she be responsive the next time he needed her to trust his decisions? The truth was, he was wondering if he deserved her trust. It was his poor judgment that had let her go into the department store in the first place. That one decision had given her pursuers the opportunity they needed. After what had happened in Florida, he was beginning to doubt his own skills as a bodyguard.

He stared at his cell phone and thought about calling Julia's father to see if he had heard from Elizabeth. He'd seen the torment etched on the older man's face when he had hugged his daughter good-bye and told Gavin,

"Take care of her." He snapped the cell phone shut. No need to call him and add to his worry needlessly. They didn't know anything for sure yet. Maybe Elizabeth had stepped out for a late night walk and didn't want her solitude broken by a ringing cell phone.

Julia opened the industrial-size refrigerator. "There's lots of food in here. Do you want a sandwich?"

"Sure." He stepped over to the wide metal counters.

Julia laid out deli ham and Swiss cheese. "This okay?"

He paced the floor. "Anything sounds good. Those donuts didn't really stay with me." Whatever explanation he came up with, he couldn't figure out what had happened to Elizabeth.

Julia took four pieces of bread out of the sack. "I know this is rude, eating Elizabeth's food without asking. But, from the way the fridge is stocked, she planned for us. Maybe we can leave a note…if we don't find her first."

Gavin weighed his options. Going back into town meant they risked being seen. Julia had been in the news enough that people might recognize her and start talking. He didn't feel comfortable leaving Julia alone in the house to search the grounds. The best choice would be to stay here for the night and stay close to Julia.

Julia stuttered in her movements as she put the bread in a toaster. "There has to be a reason why Elizabeth is gone, right?"

He nodded, trying to convince himself. He didn't want to stir her up with his concerns until he had something solid to go on. "Maybe…some kind of emergency."

After toasting the bread, she spread mustard on it.

"My mother used to make toasted ham-and-Swiss sandwiches for me when I was a little girl." Her voice was tainted with sadness.

"Your mom died when you were young?" When he was hired, he'd seen the photos in the house of a blonde little girl being hugged by her mother, but none of an older Julia with her mother.

"Cancer when I was five...after that it was just me and Dad."

She placed the sandwich on a plate and pushed it across the metal counter. She retrieved milk from the refrigerator and poured him a glass. They ate with only the sound of a ticking clock and their chewing.

She pushed her plate to one side and planted her palms on the counter, as though bracing herself for what she was about to say. "I'm sorry about...not believing you earlier when you said we needed to leave the department store."

He stared at her for a moment. Julia had freckles. He hadn't noticed that before. "It's okay." He liked the soft smile that graced her lips.

Her cheeks turned an intense red. She angled back toward the counter. "I, um...I saw some cake over here."

He'd looked at her long enough to make her self-conscious. She was so beautiful. He found himself wanting to study each of her features. "I never turn down cake."

She opened and shut cupboards until she found two dessert plates. "Why don't we go out and eat in the lobby?" After cutting the cake, she handed him a plate. "Those couches looked really comfortable and my leg is kind of hurting."

She skirted past him, accidentally brushing his back

with her arm. The soft citrus scent of the perfume she had sampled earlier surrounded him. It really did suit her. In the lobby, Julia sat down in a plush leather chair with her plate in her lap. She pulled up an ottoman to elevate her hurt leg.

After scanning the pool area for movement, Gavin chose a chair that allowed him a view of the parking lot. With as much as he had seen in the dark, the hot springs had some pluses and some minuses. The big windows on both sides of the lodge made him nervous. If the followers did locate them, it would be easy to hide in the cover of the trees, wait for Julia to walk in front of the windows and shoot her. On the other hand, the place was remote—no nosy neighbors to start talking.

Admiration colored Julia's words. "You pay attention to everything, don't you, Gavin?" The Siamese cat jumped from its perch on the chair and leapt up beside Julia.

He took a bite of cake. Rich chocolate coated his tongue. "It's my job." As far as he could tell with the limited light, only one road led into the place: a feature that was both good and bad. There was only one way for intruders to approach in a vehicle, but it also meant only one escape route for them, unless they were on foot. "I was just thinking it would be better if you didn't spend a lot of time in this room."

Julia set her cake to one side and glanced around while she petted the cat. When she thought about what the next month would be like, the walls felt as though they were closing in. "So what can I do? Do you think it would be safe for me to soak in that outdoor springs?" She fingered a beaded necklace she had around her neck.

"Maybe. I need to see the whole place in daylight

before I make those kinds of decisions." Gavin rose to his feet and paced past the window. "That library in the hot tub building probably doesn't have big windows. There might be games or table tennis or something."

The cat settled on Julia's good leg. Though he hadn't come right out and said it, his words made it clear that he preferred she stay inside…for a month. Two years of constant vigilance had left her battle weary for the final fight. She had to find a way to focus on the positive. "I brought some books, and I'm studying for my ACT. I just did my GED last month." Unwittingly, the edge had come back into her voice.

"That should keep you busy." He studied her for a moment. "Like I said, I'll know better when I can see the grounds in daylight. Maybe it's secure enough for us to go for a walk in the back. I don't know what's around us."

"Even if I can go for a walk, I won't be able to go by myself, right?" Despite her best effort at hiding it, her tone revealed frustration.

He shook his head. "We can't risk that."

"The only time I get to leave this place is when you take me to go see the lawyers to be prepped for the trial." Her voice quivered. The sensation of being trapped was like an elephant on her chest. She took in shallow, sharp breaths as memories assaulted her. In Elijah's house, there were crawl spaces with locks on the outside. Despite Marlena's protests, she'd been sent there every time she had tried to escape or had broken one of Elijah's rules. In the dark, she had clutched her knees, listened to the sound of the mice scurrying around her and prayed. Elijah had designed the punishment to break her will, but she had used it to strengthen her faith. Still, darkness and small spaces were hard for her to deal with.

Gavin turned to face her. "Look, Julia, I know you're tired of all this confinement."

"I know this is the way it has to be...for now." She picked up her plate and stabbed the cake with her fork. "I keep trying to imagine what it will be like in one month. I try to see myself outside with the sun shining down, just walking all by myself."

He moved toward her, sympathy evident in his expression. "I know this isn't easy."

She put the cat to one side and rose to her feet. "I can handle it. I am going to put Elijah in jail forever for what he did to Marlena, for the way he tried to mess with my mind and twist the word of God." Summoning courage she wasn't sure she had, she lifted her chin and squared her shoulders.

He offered her a supportive smile. "You're going to make it through this." His eyes shone with admiration.

Her chin dropped a notch. "Sometimes, though, I think about all I missed out on, and it bogs me down. I didn't learn to drive. I didn't go to the prom. I didn't go through graduation. I—" She caught herself. She couldn't go down that thought path. She tilted her head up to the second floor. *Focus on something you have control over, Julia.* "I have no idea which room I'm supposed to take."

"Why don't we go out together and get the suitcases?" He glanced toward the big windows. "I don't like the idea of you being alone in this place just yet. Then we'll figure out where you're supposed to sleep."

She walked toward the door. He grabbed her arm. "Let me go first."

Like breath on a window, the warmth of his touch

faded slowly from her arm. What was it about Gavin Shane? His proximity made her head buzz.

He slipped outside, making sure she kept pace with him. He unlocked the trunk and placed two suitcases on the gravel.

Headlights came into view at the corner of the lot. Gavin slipped in front of Julia, shielding her. He tucked his hand inside his jacket, probably where he kept his gun. Heart racing, Julia pressed close to him.

Sept. 30/21 ✓

FIVE

The car came to a stop and the headlights turned off. A woman stepped out, her face indiscernible in the darkness.

"I'm so sorry I wasn't here," the woman said. "I'm Elizabeth Johnson."

"Do you know what she looks like?" Gavin whispered in Julia's ear as the woman approached.

"Dad only had an old photograph." Julia pushed down the rising fear with a deep breath. Whoever this woman was, Gavin knew what he was doing.

The woman walked toward them with her hand out. "You must be Gavin Shane."

Julia let her guard down a little. Nothing in the older woman's demeanor suggested aggression or deviousness, and she knew Gavin's first and last name, information only her father and the police would know.

Elizabeth took a step toward Julia. "You must be Julia. Please, both of you come inside."

"We've already had a look around. I hope that was okay." Julia stepped toward Elizabeth. She didn't have to look at Gavin to know he still had his hand on the gun in his side holster. He wasn't totally convinced Elizabeth was who she said she was.

"I'm glad you made yourselves at home." Elizabeth ushered the two of them inside after they picked up their suitcases. "I wasn't going to let anything keep me from being here when you two came, but we had a little emergency. I have one man helping me with the renovations—"

"I thought the place would be unoccupied." Tension threaded through Gavin's words.

"It's all right." Elizabeth turned toward Gavin. "Steve can be trusted, and he's only here during the day. The other workers won't come until you are gone."

Gavin crossed his arms. "It really would be better if nobody knew she was here."

Elizabeth stiffened. "I assure you that Steve will not talk to anyone. I've known him for years."

Sensing rising discord, Julia interjected. "Did something happen to Steve? Was that your emergency?" She set her suitcase down.

"The man was helping me with some repairs in the horse barn and had a forgetful moment when he was using a saw." She rested her arm on the high counter with the room keys hung behind it. "I had to rush him to the emergency room…didn't even have time to grab my cell phone."

The Siamese cat came up to Elizabeth, rubbed against her leg and meowed. "I assume you've met Ophelia, the lodge cat." Elizabeth skirted around the lobby, flicking on several floor lights. The additional illumination revealed that Elizabeth was a thin woman with a tinge of color in her cheeks, a glow to her face and shoulder-length silver-white hair. She returned to Gavin and Julia.

A gasp escaped Elizabeth's lips as she turned to look at Julia in the light. She walked over and cupped Julia's face in her hands. "You are the spitting image of your mother."

"Am I?" Julia pulled away, hurt tainting her words. Talking about her mother as though she were alive re-opened old wounds. Though she didn't know why, Elizabeth's gushing kindness made her want to retreat. She wasn't sure what to think of Elizabeth.

The older woman softened her voice. "I didn't mean to be so brusque." She touched Julia's face tenderly. Her eyes glazed. "I have some wonderful stories to share about your mother."

"You have...stories about my mother?" Even as she spoke she felt the chasm in her chest, that sense of emptiness that threatened to overwhelm her. Would hearing the stories remind her not only of losing her mother, but of Marlena?

Elizabeth wrapped an arm around Julia. "Come on, I'll show you your room." She turned back around to face Gavin. "I've got a room made up for you, too, downstairs."

"Actually, I'll be planted outside Julia's door tonight." Gavin stood with his feet shoulder width apart.

Julia turned to face him. His consistent inclination toward protecting her lessoned the fear that had hovered over her for two years. "When are you going to sleep?"

Light from the chandelier played across his face and hair. "I'll catch a few hours when Elizabeth can be with you."

It had been a long day for both of them. He must be just as tired as she was. She studied him for a moment, noting the tiny scar on his cheek and the thickness of his eyelashes. Her father had done all right in hiring the bodyguard who looked more like a surfer.

* * *

Once the two women were upstairs, Gavin felt comfortable walking the grounds to get a better idea of the layout of the place. He pulled a flashlight from his suitcase.

He stepped outside, sliding the door shut. Most of the two-sided brick wall that sheltered the outdoor pool was complete, shielding it from view and making the big windows on this side of the lodge less of an issue.

To the west, beyond the cottage, was an open field and what might be the barn Elizabeth had mentioned. Old-growth forest surrounded the place to the north and south. How deep did those woods go? How many places could someone hide? He'd have to find out from Elizabeth what was behind the grounds of the hot springs. The cottonwoods continued to creak and rustle.

He sauntered around to the side of the main building. A light shone in a second-story room, and he caught a glimpse of Julia's blond head. They really needed to change her hair color. Elijah True was known for his paranoia toward the government and his stockpile of guns. No doubt he had followers with sniper skills. Julia was an easy target through that window. He'd have to talk to her about standing in front of windows and maybe even get some coverings on the lobby windows. Poor Julia would probably balk at having to live in a world that was nearly dark day and night, but it would have to be done.

In the morning, he'd be able to evaluate if they could go outside. For her emotional well-being it would be good for her to get some fresh air, but not at the risk of her safety.

Because the background checks had taken so long, Gavin had been hired last minute. He hadn't been able to

give any input on where to hide Julia. This spa wouldn't
have been his first choice, but as long as it was secure,
it would do. If the followers didn't show up in the next
couple of days, he could assume they had managed to
shake them. That was a big "if."

The full moon provided enough light for Julia to see
the tall cottonwoods swaying in the wind outside her
window.

"Make sure you twist that deadbolt," Elizabeth said.
She'd taken the time to show Julia where the fresh
towels and sheets were kept and helped Julia put away
the few clothes she had brought with her.

Julia brushed a hand over the soft lace curtain.
"Thank you."

"Well, good night. We'll visit some more tomorrow." The sound of Elizabeth shutting the door made
her wince. The memory of doors clicking shut and locks
sliding into place rushed back into her mind. Confinement had been Elijah's form of punishment. She looked
around her room decorated with quilts and lace. Inwardly, a coldness melded to her core. This was her new
prison.

When she glanced out the window a second time, she
saw Gavin walking across the grass below. He seemed
intent on a purpose, focused on his surroundings. Something about him was like a lion ready to pounce, yet he
seemed to have an inner calm.

As ordered, Julia deadbolted her door. She retrieved
her pajamas from her suitcase, brushed her teeth and
folded back the covers. She pulled the quilt up to her
shoulders and stared at the ceiling. She was unbeliev-
ably tired, but wasn't sure if she would be able to sleep.
Her father's fears had not been unfounded. As the trial

grew closer, staying at the house would have put her in danger. At least they didn't know she was here at the hot springs. But she missed her father already. In the morning when she could manage a calm voice, she would call him.

Gavin's professionalism helped ease the constant fear about the followers being around every corner. It was as if he carried some of her burden, lifting her anxiety.

The doorknob shook.

Heart racing, she sat upright.

"Julia, sorry to bother you, but you have locked the door." Gavin spoke softly.

Julia flipped back the covers, charged across the room and slid back the deadbolt. "Elizabeth said to lock the door." She tried to keep the irritation out of her voice. All these contradictory orders.

A smile crossed Gavin's face. "Elizabeth isn't a security expert. At night when I am outside your door, it would be better to leave it unlocked in case I have to rush in here." He indicated the chair he would be sitting on. "If I have to leave for any reason, lock your door."

She let out a heavy sigh. "That makes sense." And it made her feel less claustrophobic to have the door unlocked.

He stepped into her room and checked the window to make sure it was latched. "Don't stand in front of this for any length of time."

"I'll try to be aware of that." She hung her head. "Sorry I was so obstinate a moment ago."

"It's okay." He leaned toward her, placed his hand on her jaw and lifted her chin. His wide brown eyes held an honesty that was reassuring. "Elizabeth is only trying to be helpful. I'm the one you need to listen to. I'll keep you safe."

Julia opened her mouth to respond, but the intensity of his expression left her speechless.

He pulled away. "I'll be right out here."

Julia's heart thudded as the door eased shut. Her skin tingled all over. His touch had that kind of effect on her. She let out a huff of air. If he wanted to have a business relationship, he was going to have to quit doing that kind of stuff. Now she wasn't going to be able to sleep.

She grabbed the ACT study guide and collapsed in the leather chair in the corner. She read for a few minutes. Brushing her hands over the pages of the booklet, the image of the woman in the coffee shop came back into her head. Her heart ached as she tried to picture herself at that same table with her book open, sipping a coffee.

Someday, Julia, someday.

After the trial, she could go to college. She'd stroll carefree across a campus, meeting friends, sitting in a class taking notes. Normal things would happen. She'd meet someone, and they'd fall in love.

Outside, Gavin's chair scraped across the floor.

Gavin leaned his chair back against the wall, crossing his legs at the ankle and resting them on the railing.

Down below, Elizabeth came into view when she emerged from the dining hall. She peered up at him as she wiped her hands on a dishrag. "I'm going to head back to my place, unless you need me to stay. I'm not sure how this whole thing is supposed to work."

"That's fine for tonight. Maybe tomorrow it would be a good idea for you to sleep in the lodge in the room next to Julia's. We'll figure it out in the morning." He still wasn't sure what to think of Elizabeth or her story about the emergency. He wondered if William had run any kind of check on her, or had just taken her at her word.

He drew his attention back to Julia's door. A thought occurred to him. "Hey, Elizabeth." He walked down the stairs. "Do you know anything about perfume?"

Elizabeth furled her brow. "Perfume?"

"Julia picked some out for herself earlier, and she wasn't able to get it." He gave her the short, cleaned-up version of what had happened. "I don't know what it was called. It smelled kind of like—"

"Oranges and lemons. I smelled it when I hugged her. I think I know which one it is. I can get it for her tomorrow."

"Thank you." It wouldn't be the same as going to a counter and buying it herself, but she had picked it out.

Elizabeth studied Gavin for a moment. "That's kind of a personal thing to give a woman."

Heat rose up his neck. "I didn't mean it that way. The perfume is a...sort of symbol of freedom to her. I just thought it would help with the frustration she feels about the confinement and give her hope about a normal future."

"I can get it for her then." Elizabeth pointed toward the sliding glass doors. "I'll go out that way. You can latch it behind me."

Once Elizabeth was gone, Gavin latched the sliding door and then checked all the other locks. This place didn't even have an alarm system. Not the best setup, but he was going to have to work with it. Moving Julia again would produce a whole new set of hazards, and as far as he knew, this place was secret.

Gavin headed back up the stairs. He hadn't expected

to be drawn to Julia like this. He'd seen the flash of attraction in her eyes when he'd touched her cheek. He'd
crossed a line. He'd given his word to her father. That
couldn't happen again.

Once on the balcony, he pulled his gun from his side
holster and placed it on a table that had a lamp on it. He
scooted the table closer and situated his chair.

He'd taken this job because being a bodyguard
was what he'd done since he was eighteen. Until he'd
watched a friend who'd hired him get shot in front
of him, he had thought he was good at his job. He'd
grown up with Joshua Van Dyken. Both of them had
been adrenaline junkies when they were teenagers, but
Joshua was the one who had done something with his
skill and become a race-car driver. They'd met up again
when both of them lived in Florida and Joshua had hired
him as his bodyguard.

Gavin's hesitation and decision to step to the right
instead of the left had given the crazed fan the opportunity he'd been looking for. Joshua had recovered, but the
gunshot wound had done nerve damage and affected his
reflexes. Joshua would live, but he wouldn't race again.
Racked with guilt, Gavin hadn't spoken to him since the
shooting. Seeing his friend unconscious in a hospital
bed had torn him to pieces. He'd ended up in the hospital chapel asking God for help. The one good thing
that had come out of Florida was a renewed faith.

Gavin closed his eyes and prayed for an uneventful
night, for the stirred-up feelings about the past to go
away. This praying stuff was going to take a while to
get used to. He opened his eyes and stared down at the
quiet lobby below as Ophelia stretched, arched her back
and settled in her spot.

The shooting with Joshua in Florida had shaken his

confidence. And now, after today's blunder in the department store, he was beginning to wonder if he was the best man to protect Julia.

SIX

A cry from inside Julia's room woke Gavin from his half slumber. In a single swift movement, he jerked to his feet, grabbed his gun, swung around and tapped on the door. "Julia?"

"I'm fine. It's just…my leg." She sounded like she was in pain.

He clasped the doorknob. An urgency to be with her, to make sure she was okay, pressed on him. "May I come in?"

"Yes, please."

When Gavin opened the door, Julia was slumped down in the chair beside the bed. Her face was drained of color.

He put the gun back in his side holster and rushed over to her.

"I took a shower and got dressed." She turned her leg slightly. "It hurts worse."

The sight of the blood-stained bandage sent a chill through him.

"Can I look?"

She nodded. "I taped plastic over it. I thought it would be okay to take a shower. When I took the plastic off, it was bleeding again."

Taking care not to pull too hard, he peeled back the bandage. He winced. He'd dressed the wound so quickly. Maybe the cut was more severe than he had first thought.

She sucked air through her teeth. "How does it look?"

"I'm going to touch around the cut. You tell me if it hurts." As gently as he could, he pressed his finger into her skin about an inch from the gash.

She jerked her leg. "Yup, that hurts."

"It's not red yet, but maybe it's the start of an infection. We need to get you to a doctor. You might need stitches. I don't want to take any chances of this turning into a full-blown infection."

"How are we going to manage that?" Her voice trembled from the pain. "Doctors don't make house calls anymore."

They were both thinking the same thing. She'd have to go out in public again. That meant risking cult members coming out of the woodwork. Realistically, they couldn't be everywhere. But it wasn't just Elijah's followers he was worried about. Julia's face had been plastered across newspapers after her escape. If she was recognized, people would start talking and word would get back to the followers, or worse, some local Clark Kent would decide doing a story on her was his big break.

"It takes about twenty-four hours for infection to set in. Elizabeth might have something to help manage the pain, and I bet she knows of a doctor that would be low risk in terms of lots of people seeing you."

"I could dye my hair sunset red, if that would help. You said my blond hair is too easy to see at a distance."

"Do you feel strong enough to stand over a sink?"

"Elizabeth can help me." Her lower lip quivered, and her fingers dug into the arms of the chair.

"I'll find out if she knows of a doctor who won't be a liability." Gavin's heart lurched. He could see that she was hurting, and he longed to be able to just wipe it away. "Sit tight." He ran down the stairs. The banging of pots and pans came from the kitchen as the heady scent of bacon cooking greeted him.

He pushed through the doors past the dining room, into the kitchen. Elizabeth, dressed in a flowery apron, divided scrambled eggs on to three plates. "Oh, good, is Julia up?"

"She cut her leg yesterday. It's bleeding again." It wasn't necessary to explain how she had gotten the injury.

Elizabeth set the spatula on the counter. "I noticed her jeans were torn last night. What can I do to help?"

"We need to have a doctor look at it. Do you know a doctor who's not going to make treating Julia part of his dinner conversation and who won't ask a lot of questions?"

"I know just the man." Elizabeth stepped away from the counter and placed her hands on her hips. "It's a bit of a drive to get to him, about fifty miles."

"Actually, it would be best if he was far away instead of in Silver Cliff. If Julia is spotted, I want it to be hard to link her back to this place. If you give me the number, I'll make the call."

"All these precautions." Elizabeth's hands dropped to her side, and she drew her lips into a tight line. "This is very serious, isn't it? I read the stories in the newspapers." She shook her head. "But I had no idea what Julia was dealing with on a day-to-day basis."

"I assumed Julia's father explained exactly what was involved." Gavin stamped down his irritation. If he hadn't been brought in so late in the process, Elizabeth would've been fully briefed on the need for tight security.

"All he said was that he didn't feel like she was safe at his home." She wiped her hands on her apron and turned to face him. "Don't get me wrong, I'm glad I'm here to help out."

"Do you have any first-aid supplies? Her cut probably needs to be dressed again. And if you have anything to help manage the pain, that would be great."

"No problem. I have all those things around for guests." Elizabeth opened a drawer and pulled out a piece of paper and a pen. "Let me write down Doctor Severson's number and directions to his place." Her pen whirled across the paper and then she handed it to him.

"Thanks." He stared at the number. "I'm going to make up a cover, just to be safe."

"I'm sure he can be trusted, but it's a good idea to be extra cautious," Elizabeth said. "And mentioning my name should be enough to not make him ask any questions." The seriousness of the threat against Julia seemed to be sinking in for Elizabeth.

"Also, we are going to dye her hair before we leave. Can you give her a hand with that?"

"Yes, I can do that." She wiped her hands on the apron and shook her head. "That poor girl." She retrieved a first-aid kit out of the drawer and left the kitchen.

Maybe now that Elizabeth understood the need to be overly careful, she wouldn't be so gung-ho about her handyman coming around. Gavin wandered into the lobby to make the call. Upstairs, he could hear the two women laughing and water running.

As he dialed the doctor's number, he stared through the large glass doors past the outdoor pool. There was a light dusting of snow on the ground, and just beyond Elizabeth's little cabin was a barn and a corral. Two horses trotted around their winter pasture. The barn was fairly large. More horses were probably inside. Elizabeth must provide them for guests.

Gavin tensed as the phone rang for the fifth time. What option did they have if this guy wasn't around?

"Hello, Doctor Severson's office." The voice on the other end of the line sounded like that of an older man.

"Dr. Severson?" He hadn't expected the doctor to answer the phone.

"Yes, that's me."

"You don't have a receptionist?"

"Nah, she's out of commission for a month or so. She just had a baby. Seven pounds, eight ounces, beautiful baby boy. Don't want to hire a temp. So I got to hold down the fort myself."

The doctor had a folksy way of talking. No receptionist was a good thing, it meant one less person to recognize Julia. Gavin cleared his throat. He needed a cover that sounded believable. "My wife and I are staying at Elizabeth Johnson's place."

"Oh, really? I thought she closed up for the winter to get some repairs done." The comment sounded more chatty than suspicious.

Gavin scrambled for an explanation that made sense. "She made an exception for us. We're on our honeymoon."

"Oh, I see. Any friend of Elizabeth's is a friend of mine. What can I help you with?"

Though mentioning they were staying at the hot springs could be viewed as a breach in security, Elizabeth had been right about her name sweeping away any suspicion. The doctor probably wouldn't ask any more questions. "My wife has cut herself on a piece of metal. I'm concerned about infection."

"Metal? Did you happen to notice if it was rusty? She might need a tetanus shot."

Gavin shifted his weight. "Can I bring her in?"

"Sure, I'm keeping a light patient load until Lindsey gets back, but if you're staying with Elizabeth, I sure don't mind helping her out. Let me check the schedule." There was a pause on the line. Gavin detected shuffling of papers and the sound of a computer being turned on. "How about three o'clock this afternoon?"

"I'll get her there." Gavin hung up the phone and paced. He stared out the window at the long strip of flat land. Unless someone snuck up through the trees, he would at least see them coming from a long ways away. The brick wall that was almost complete around the outdoor pool provided cover, making it safe for Julia to soak.

Upstairs he heard water running. Elizabeth appeared at the top of the stairs. "Julia's almost done." She came down. "Those eggs are probably cold by now, but it's food. I can warm them in the microwave. Let me get them for you."

Elizabeth left the lobby and returned a few minutes later. After handing Gavin his plate and setting Julia's on the check-in counter, she grabbed her own plate and stood close to Gavin.

"You've had a look around." She took a bite of eggs. "Does this place meet your needs?"

"In some ways, yes. There is no alarm system. Julia and I will need keys to the doors, and we need to make sure they're locked at all times."

Elizabeth nodded. "I can do that."

Gavin pointed through the sliding glass doors. "What's on the back end of your property?"

"I have a huge buffer of acreage around me. People have to ask permission to come on the land."

Gavin doubted the followers would ask permission for anything if they located this place. It was reassuring, though, to know Elizabeth didn't have any close neighbors.

"There might be a little town way on the other side of my land. I assure you, Mr. Shane, this place is remote." Elizabeth finished her breakfast and excused herself, saying she had to get some things done.

Gavin had nearly finished his eggs when Julia came to the top of the stairs.

She turned her head side to side. "What do you think of me as a redhead?"

She was stunning no matter what color her hair was. He walked to the bottom of the stairs. "It'll work."

She came down and stood close to him. "So you like it." The difference in hair color made her eyes seem even bluer. Nothing would change her angelic features. She might still be recognized close up, but at least she wouldn't be spotted at a distance.

"You look good as a redhead." He reached up and touched the soft ends of it. "How would you feel about braiding it or putting it up in some way?" All the newspaper photos had been of her with long, free-flowing hair.

She pulled back, eyes turning to stone. "No."

He'd struck a nerve. "I'm sorry. If you want your hair long..."

"It's not that." She turned her head away and gripped the banister. "It's just that Elijah required all the women to have their hair up in tight braids." She turned to face him, blue eyes filled with emotion. "I won't ever do that again. I know it's dumb, but it's too much of a reminder."

"It's not dumb, Julia." He hadn't heard fear in her voice, but resolve, as though she had put her foot down against the past controlling her. "You have a very distinctive face. The less we can make you look like you, the better. Would you be okay with cutting it?"

She combed through the hair and drew a coppery strand of it in front of her eyes. "I guess I would be okay with that. If that's what we have to do."

"We can grab one of those stools over there. Elizabeth probably has scissors somewhere." He searched the drawers of the check-in desk. When he looked up, Julia was limping across the floor. "You just sit down and relax. I'll get the chair."

"I can handle it." She picked up the stool and, with her free hand, pushed on the sliding glass door. The determination he heard in her tone told him that she didn't like being pitied. "Outside would be best, huh? It's a pretty warm day and clean up will probably be easier."

His head jerked up, and he cast a furtive glance to the wide expanse of land behind the pool. Outside would also be riskier. "Yeah, sure." He couldn't keep her inside all the time. Loss of freedom made her wither emotionally. He had to find the balance between protecting her physically and making sure she didn't shut down because of the confinement. "Position the stool so it's hidden behind the brick wall."

Julia offered him a smile. "There you go again, doing your job."

"Was I that obvious?" He found two pairs of scissors in an upper drawer.

"Get rid of that worried look. I need to feel the sun on my face. I know I'll be safe if you're out here with me."

She sure had a lot confidence in his abilities. He picked up the scissors that looked sharper and walked toward the open door.

Julia settled on the stool. "Besides, they don't know I'm here, right?"

On instinct, Gavin scanned the perimeter around him, taking a mental photograph of each point his gaze landed on. It was his job to assume that they were always vulnerable. A single moment of dropping his guard could spell disaster. He cringed. Or one bad decision could lead to Julia's death.

And that would be something he'd never recover from.

Julia stared at him. Just the hint of fear clouded the composure he had seen in her expression a moment before. "They don't know where I am, right?" she repeated.

He had to be careful not to frighten her. She had had enough of that to last a lifetime. "You don't need to worry about that, Julia. That's my job." He rested his hands on her shoulders. "We were extremely careful about shaking them yesterday."

The stiffness in her posture disappeared. "That's good to hear." She pointed to the scissors. "Have you done this before?"

"Yes."

"From hair stylist to bodyguard, quite the transition."

He liked her quick wit. "Actually, the hair cutting occurred as part of my work. Think about it—when you describe someone, isn't hair one of the first things you talk about."

"It does become part of your identity, doesn't it?" She grabbed her long hair twisted it and flipped it over her shoulder. "I guess it has to go. Maybe it will help give me a new identity."

"Tilt your head back and close your eyes." His fingers grazed her temple as he pulled the hair away from her head. Her hair was soft to the touch. He circled around her, cutting quickly. Sunlight played across her face. He studied the angle of her cheekbones and the narrowness of her nose.

She must have felt him staring because she opened her eyes. "Does it look okay?"

He stepped back to escape the magnetic allure of her eyes. He found himself craving being physically close to her. "It looks all right." His gaze dropped to her lips. He dismissed the fleeting thought of kissing her and cleared his throat. Where had that come from?

It was just because she was beautiful. Then again, he had guarded beautiful women before and never had to battle these feelings. There was something different about Julia.

She tilted her head and looked up at him. "I guess I'll have to wait until I can look in the mirror."

"It's not as good as a professional job, but it will do." He reminded himself of the promise he had made to Julia's father. It'd been an easy promise to make before he had met Julia. He hadn't counted on the way she made him feel all turned around inside, just by being in the same room with her.

In his profession, women, especially women he guarded, tended to throw themselves at him, a quality that repelled him. Julia's reserved behavior was refreshing. There was much to like about her.

She pulled the shorter strand of hair out over her forehead. "Do you like it?"

Again he was struck by the contradiction in Julia's life. There was something almost naive in the way she talked to him, and yet he saw a maturity and an understanding that had grown from having faced so much trauma. "I think it looks just fine." He leaned back toward her. "I've got a little more left to cut in the front, if you'll close your eyes for me."

He didn't know quite how to navigate through that contradiction in Julia's personality. Her innocence made him feel a need to protect her that went beyond his job description. He hadn't seen any of the fragility Julia's father had alluded to. What he saw was determination. But if her father said Julia was fragile, then Julia was fragile. A promise was a promise.

Julia closed her eyes. Gavin's fingertips warmed her skin as they brushed over her temple, and he pulled a strand of hair up and away from her head. His feet padded lightly on the concrete of the patio, moving around her and then cutting the strand close to her face. He stood close enough for her to feel the softness of his breath on her cheek.

The lightheadedness she had felt yesterday returned. The counselor had explained to her that in many ways she was still thirteen. The captivity had halted the natural maturing that was supposed to happen during those years. She had been playing catch up ever since. She told herself she was ready to face anything, but sometimes she wasn't so sure.

Dating hadn't even been on the radar. She'd been focused on college and just having a circle of friends. Gavin was an attractive man, but she could sense him becoming guarded. He had probably dated lots of women. What could he possibly see in her, she had so much to learn, to experience. She really had to let go of these blossoming feelings.

He moved around to the back of the stool, drawing out a strand by her neck and snipping. "I'll just take a couple inches off back here."

"You can cut off more if you want. I'm warming to the idea of short hair." Something about letting go of the long blond hair that had made Elijah see her as angelic appealed to her. It was one more way she could make a break with the terror she had lived under for so many years.

"I heard you and Elizabeth laughing earlier when she was helping you with your hair. She seems like a good person." He cut some more strands and then moved around to the other side.

"She's okay." As kind as Elizabeth was, Julia had felt herself pulling away when she was around the older woman. No need to form attachments. This arrangement was temporary. Elizabeth would exit her life, too.

"Hey, what's that about?" Gavin's voice, flushed with compassion, pulled her from her thoughts. His thumb wiped away the single tear that had formed and trailed down her cheek. His face was close to hers when she opened her eyes.

She leaned back. She'd been so deep in thought, the tear had come spontaneously. She hadn't had time to register how thinking about the past made her sad. "Can we talk about something else?" The emotion was so raw. She had to fight the desire to run to her room and bury her face in a pillow.

Gavin smiled. "Sure, what do you want to talk about?"

The sound of approaching footsteps caused both of them to turn toward the trees. A man appeared from behind the half-built wall, holding something in his hand.

Julia had no time to register fear before Gavin had gathered her in his arms and pulled her toward the open door.

SEVEN

"Get down, away from the window." Gavin let go of Julia and drew his pistol out of the side holster, seeking cover out of view of the window.

Julia scrambled to a corner of the lobby and sank to the floor. Gavin rolled along the wall and peeked out the sliding glass doors to get a read on where the man was. He scanned right to left. The man was gone.

Gavin latched the sliding glass door. Julia was still huddled in a corner. "Stay low. Get to a room where you can lock the door and stay there until you hear my voice."

Julia was obviously stunned, but she nodded and, crouching, headed toward a first-floor room. With his gun still drawn, Gavin moved lightly and quickly to the front door.

He reached out to lock the front door when the doorknob shook. He pressed against the wall out of view, ready to fire if he had to. The door swung open. Elizabeth stepped in, and she raised her hands. An expression of terror filled her features when she saw Gavin.

Gavin dropped the gun to his side. "Don't ever do that again. Identify yourself before you open the door."

Elizabeth still hadn't regained her composure. "Steve

didn't mean...he didn't mean to scare you. He came and got me."

Steve, the man they'd seen outside, stood behind Elizabeth.

Gavin tried to shake off the rising anger. "Why didn't you tell us to expect him?"

"I didn't know he was coming. With his injury, he couldn't do much work. He just came to get some tools to loan to a friend. He didn't know you were here."

Steve stepped forward. He was an older man with hair graying at the temple. The "something" Gavin had registered as being in Steve's hand was the thick bandage he wore around his fingers and wrist.

"I'll get my tools," said Steve. "Elizabeth has explained things to me. I'm not going to talk."

How was he going to protect Julia if Elizabeth turned this place into Grand Central Station? Gavin spoke through gritted teeth. "It would be better if he didn't come around at all."

Steve threw up his hands. "Look, sorry for all the trouble. I'll get my tools and go." He disappeared around the corner of the lodge.

"Steve knowing we are here raises serious issues." His anger faded when he saw how upset Elizabeth was. He lowered his voice. "I didn't mean to scare you like that."

"It's okay. You were only doing your job." She patted her chest to indicate that her heart was slowing down. "I assure you, Julia will be safe here."

"Not if people keep showing up unannounced," Gavin said. "Someone knows she's here. We might have to move her."

"Please, I haven't compromised her safety. Steve is trustworthy." Elizabeth grabbed Gavin's arm. "She needs to stay here. I want to get to know her." Her voice softened. "I think she needs me."

"She hasn't exactly warmed to you."

"I know that, and I didn't expect her to right away, after all the loss she has suffered. But I'm asking you, for Julia's sake, give me the chance to reach out to her."

Gavin shook his head and stared at the door where Julia had locked herself in. "I don't know. Both the doctor and Steve know we are here. Some aspects of this place are less than ideal." He wrestled with his options. The remoteness, the buffer of land around them and the fact that so far the location was unknown to the followers were marks in the plus column.

Elizabeth leveled her eyes at Gavin. "Neither of those two men will talk. I give you my word. I won't do anything that puts her in danger."

Elizabeth's sincerity touched him. Julia still had some wounds she needed to work through. The tear he had seen earlier revealed that. Maybe another woman could reach her in a way he couldn't. "I've got to get Julia to the doctor. We'll talk about this when I get back."

She grabbed his shirt sleeve. "Can we please just be on the same team for Julia, to want the best for her?"

"I do want the best for her. It won't matter that you guys become best buddies if she's dead," Gavin said.

Elizabeth took a step back. Her voice grew even softer. "It could take weeks to find another safe place."

"I know that." Gavin headed up the stairs to get Julia. Taking her out in the open had already been proven to be fraught with risk.

"Like you said, we can talk about it when you get back." She turned away.

When Gavin was halfway across the floor, Julia opened the door and stepped out. The lack of color in her features could be because of her leg, or it could be because she had overheard the conversation. In any case, she had had way more excitement than she needed.

"Is everything okay?" Her voice trembled.

"False alarm. It was just Elizabeth's handyman," said Gavin. "Let's get you to the doctor."

A few minutes later, Julia got into the passenger side of the SUV. Gavin held her arm to boost her up and keep her from putting weight on the injured leg.

He leaned into the car window. "You doing okay?"

She nodded. Elizabeth stood in the doorway with her arms crossed. Julia hadn't been able to hear the content of the conversation between Elizabeth and Gavin, but it had sounded heated. Gavin got behind the steering wheel and put the key in the ignition.

Julia's nerves were raw from everything that had happened. She drew a bag filled with glass beads out of her purse and strung the beads on the silk thread she had brought.

Gavin shifted into reverse and turned around in the gravel lot. "What are you making?"

"A necklace. It was one of the things the counselor and I came up with to deal with anxiety." She felt as though she had been shaken from the inside.

"So it's like therapy." His voice softened. He turned on to the two-lane road that intersected the dirt road. "You certainly had enough happen this morning to stress you out."

Julia closed her eyes and massaged her temple. "I just don't like it when people fight about me."

"That bothered you more than Steve showing up and us having to dive inside?"

The truth was, even though the incident had made her heart race, she had felt completely safe with Gavin close. He knew what he was doing. If she just listened to him, she would be fine. "In a way, yes."

Marlena had fought with Elijah all the time. Julia would be awakened by the shouting late at night. Marlena had been the only cult member who knew Julia had been kidnapped. At first, the fights were about just leaving Julia on a street and hoping she didn't remember enough to press charges. When Elijah refused, Marlena's attachment to Julia grew. Later, the fights became about finding a husband for Julia so she would feel more like a part of the "community."

"I'm sorry you had to hear us fighting. I like Elizabeth. I think she cares about you. It's just that I don't know if the hot springs is the best location."

She pulled a glass bead out of the bag, pressing her fingers hard against it. She had felt more trusting toward Elizabeth, too. "I don't want to move again. I can't run anymore like we had to do on the way here."

Gavin adjusted his sunglasses. "The lodge has some things going for it."

"There is no indication that they know where I am." Julia yanked the bead she'd picked out to the bottom of the strand. "They would have come into the house to get me by now."

"You're right about that. I do think we shook them off before we got to the springs."

"And I would appreciate it if you and Elizabeth would try to get along."

"I only want you to be as safe as possible," he said.

"Can we please just stay at the hot springs for now?

I don't know how to explain it, but when I have to stay on the run, it feels like Elijah is still controlling me." The raw, unexpected pain was evident in her voice.

He drove without responding for several minutes. "This is your life we're talking about, Julia. It's in my hands and I want to do this right."

"I just think leaving would bring on more trouble than staying here. Besides, you're doing just fine keeping me safe." She had been impressed with Gavin so far. She needed to call her father and thank him for hiring him. "My father said you guarded some really important people when you were down in Florida."

Julia noticed a subtle change in Gavin's expression, as if a veil had fallen over his eyes. He looked forward and focused on his driving. "Why don't you read those directions that Elizabeth wrote down?"

He really didn't like her asking questions about his life, especially about his time in Florida—yet another indication that he saw her as just a client whom he didn't want to get too close to.

Julia unfolded the note Elizabeth had written. The tension that had entered the vehicle was palpable. Maybe she could lighten the mood. "Here we are again, you driving and me navigating, like some old married couple," she blurted. Mentally, Julia kicked herself. What had made her say such an immature-sounding thing? She might as well just write "Julia loves Gavin" in her school notebook. "I, um, didn't mean it that way."

He angled his head and offered her a smile. "Mean it what way?"

"I was thirteen when Elijah took me. I never got a chance to go on dates." She turned sideways and stared at the scenery. "I missed out on that whole learning to talk to boys thing. Sometimes I say the wrong thing." The ache around her heart returned.

"It didn't bother me." He seemed amused.

Julia focused on stringing beads on her necklace. Though he was maybe five or six years older than her, he would never view her as an equal. Maybe that was why she had a sense he was keeping emotional distance.

"So why don't you read those directions for me?"

Julia unfolded the piece of paper. "About half a block after the town welcome sign, you'll see a white building set off by itself."

"That's good. Sounds like it's on the outskirts of town."

"Less chance of someone noticing me. Is that what you are thinking?"

Something like admiration flashed through his eyes. "Exactly."

"There it is." Julia pointed. "That has to be it."

When Gavin pulled into the lot there were two other vehicles, a battered-looking truck and a compact car. An open field and a closed gas station separated the doctor's office from the rest of the town. They could get Julia treated and leave without having to cross paths with hardly anyone.

Gavin jumped out of the vehicle and circled around to help Julia out. She was limping even more. He took her arm and placed it on his shoulder. The trust he saw in her eyes floored him. Did he deserve that trust?

"If anyone asks, you and I are husband and wife."

"We are?"

"Just for our cover. That's why I thought it was funny

when you said we were acting like husband and wife in the car."

"Oh, I understand." She slipped past him while he held the door.

When they got inside, a middle-aged woman and her teenage daughter were sitting in the waiting room.

An older man with thinning hair combed against his head looked up from the chart he had been reading at a high desk. "Are you the gentleman who called earlier?"

Gavin nodded, appreciating that the doctor hadn't dropped any specific information in front of the other people in the waiting room.

The doctor pulled his glasses off his collar where he had hung them. "I understand you cut your leg. So sad to have this happen on your honeymoon."

Julia raised an eyebrow toward Gavin. "Yes, that's what happened." She spoke without taking her eyes off him.

"Just right this way into exam room one." The doctor addressed Julia.

Automatically, Gavin trailed behind them.

The doctor narrowed his eyes. "I know you are just married, but I'm sure your wife can handle being in the exam room alone."

Gavin backed away, not wanting to call attention to how closely he watched her, but dreading being separated from her. "I'll just be in the next room…honey."

"Okay…honey." Amusement danced through her eyes as she looked back at him and entered the exam room.

Julia lifted her pant leg. "I didn't think it was that bad, but it started bleeding again."

Just as he turned to leave, Gavin heard the doctor

say, "Doesn't look bad enough for stitches." The doctor closed the exam-room door.

While Julia was with the doctor Gavin flipped through a magazine, but he barely paid attention to it. Though he maintained a surface calm, agitation stirred underneath. He didn't like being where he couldn't see her. The waiting room had a small window where he could take note of vehicles pulling into the lot.

"Did your wife hurt her leg?" The middle-aged woman smiled pleasantly. Her teenage daughter slumped down in the chair and rested her chin on her chest.

They must be doing a good job of convincing people they were a couple. "She's got a bad cut."

"I noticed she was kind of limping."

"Yes, it's causing some pain." Gavin feigned interest in his magazine. He didn't want to give out any more information than he had to. While he waited, a woman who was probably in her mid-forties came in and sat down. Her hair was pulled back into a tight bun. Lack of makeup made her pale features look even more washed out. She sat straight as a board in the chair opposite Gavin. Something about the woman was off-putting.

Outside, he heard a car peel through the parking lot. The sooner he could get Julia back to the hot springs, the better.

Twenty minutes later, Julia emerged from the exam room, still favoring her leg, but the color had come back into her face.

She held up a piece of paper. "I have to get some antibiotics to prevent infection."

"We can get—" He caught himself before he said Elizabeth's name. "Somebody else to get the pills."

On the way out to the SUV Gavin noted that two cars went by, slowing down to stare at them as he helped

Julia back into the vehicle. Could just be because it was a small town, and they were not locals. All the same, he made a mental note of the make and model of the cars.

Julia exuded renewed energy. "He put a waterproof bandage on so I can still soak in the hot springs. I will be able to do that, right?"

He wrestled with finding a balance between confining her to a dark room with no light and giving her enough freedom so she didn't go stir crazy. The pool with the wall around it was pretty secure. Steve had come around because he knew the layout of the place. Anyone else would probably go to the front first. "It would be best if I stood watch while you did." He turned the key in the ignition.

"Thank you," she said sincerely.

Gavin checked the rearview mirror on a regular basis. Only one car, which passed them when Gavin slowed, was on the road. As he drove, he realized how tired he was. He had slept in short intervals and not very deeply while he was posted outside Julia's door. All he needed was a couple hours of deep sleep to feel revived.

Elizabeth was dusting in the lobby when they arrived. She straightened, massaging the small of her back. "I've talked to Steve. Even if he is feeling well enough to work, he won't be around until after you two are gone."

"Thank you. If you don't mind, I'm going to catch a couple hours of shut-eye," Gavin said.

"I can help Elizabeth dust," Julia offered.

"Remember, I said it would be better if you didn't spend too much time in front of those big windows."

"It's always something." Julia's voice held a hint of

teasing. He was glad to see she had decided to have a sense of humor about the precautions they had to take.

Elizabeth said, "I've got some books in our little library that need to be alphabetized. The room only has a small, high window. We can work on that."

The gravity of the threat they faced seemed to finally be sinking in for Elizabeth. At least she was willing to make adjustments. Her concern for Julia's emotional well-being went a long way for Gavin trusting her.

"I'll leave you two ladies alone for a while then." He trudged across the lobby to the first-floor room Elizabeth had made up for him that he hadn't even seen yet.

Gavin kicked off his boots, pulled back the covers and fell into bed. Sleep came quickly. His last thought was that he regretted that he had to sleep at all. Elizabeth seemed to be gaining an understanding of the need for vigilance but, given the level of danger Julia faced, he would feel better if he could stay close to her twenty-four hours a day.

EIGHT

Julia pushed open the sliding glass door. Dressed in a lush spa robe Elizabeth had loaned her and a swimsuit, the winter cold hit her full on. The collision of the heat from the pool and cold air formed steam on the surface of the water.

Elizabeth had already settled into the outdoor pool. "The hot water feels so good this time of year." She leaned back and stared at the night sky. "I love being in the winter chill and then easing into the springs."

It was barely six o'clock and already dark. Elizabeth and Julia had spent the afternoon organizing the library that was in a tiny room in the building that housed the indoor hot tubs. After some kitchen cleanup and a light dinner, Elizabeth had talked her into a soak in the tub, assuring her that it was safe and that there was no need to wake Gavin from the sleep he so obviously needed.

Steam rose off the outdoor pool as Julia eased in, slipping down until the water covered her shoulders. The water was not more than five feet deep. "How long have you owned this place?"

Elizabeth stared up at the night sky, allowing her legs to float out in front of her. "Twenty-five years. Brian and I raised our two children while we ran the place.

After Brian died, I decided I was just too old to make any big changes, so I just kept running it."

"That's a long time to stay in one place." How wonderful would it be to be settled, to call a place home and to feel safe there?

"Your mother came here once when you were really little," Elizabeth said.

"Really?" Julia felt an unexpected spark of interest. In a way, she had closed the emotional door on her mother, even more so after Marlena died.

"It was shortly after we bought the place. You were maybe two years old." Elizabeth planted her feet on the bottom of the pool and glided toward Julia as the water swished around her. "She loved you so much."

Her dad had told her the same thing. The memories of her mother were faint at best. She'd seen the pictures of her mother holding her. She had no memory of being loved, only that people told her she had been. Her clearest memories of her mother were of her always saying she was tired and needed to sleep.

"I'm so sorry I didn't stay in touch after she died. You just get busy with life and you lose sight of what matters." A moment of silence passed, as though Elizabeth were processing an abundance of memories. A laugh escaped her lips. "I'll tell you one thing. Your mother was a wild one in high school."

The revelation surprised Julia. "Dad never said anything about that."

"William met Hannah after she calmed down and found the Lord."

Elizabeth let out a sigh. "Your mother loved to dive off high cliffs into deep water. She loved horses. I had such a hard time keeping up with her when we went horseback riding."

"My mom rode horses?"

"Child, your mother was a champion barrel racer."

This was a side of her mother that Julia knew nothing about.

"You know, I think I still have some of the photographs from high school in our store room. It wouldn't take me but a minute to find them." Elizabeth stood up.

"I'd like that." Her curiosity piqued, the trepidation she had felt about learning more about her mother was gone.

Elizabeth pulled herself out of the springs. "You're going to want to get out in a few minutes to cool down. We can look at the photos then. I'll go find them." She grabbed her robe and walked to the sliding glass door.

Julia closed her eyes and rested her head against the back of the pool. She could hear the water from the underground spring feeding into the pool and the creaking of the trees as the wind stirred. When she opened her eyes, the fog on the water's surface made it hard to see even a foot in front of her. Her heart beat a little faster. Gavin probably wouldn't be happy to know she was out here by herself. Elizabeth had only left for a minute.

Julia dove under, allowing the warm water to envelope her. She came up on the other side of the pool. She thought she heard something that sounded like a footstep. She turned, unable to see more than a few inches in front of her through the fog. She wasn't even sure what direction the sound had come from. She had the sensation that someone was watching her.

She shook her head. She just wasn't used to being alone like this: that was why she was panicked. Unbidden, images crashed through her mind. The memory of being shoved into a dark, small cubbyhole, of the door slamming and locking, invaded her thoughts. Elijah would leave her in there for hours until she heard the bolt slide and saw the pinhole light from a flashlight. Then Marlena would finally gather her into her arms.

Still unable to shake off the anxiety the vivid memories produced, Julia turned a half circle in the pool as the water rippled around her. She still couldn't see much through the fog. She swam to the edge and pulled herself out.

She stared into the empty lobby. Where was Elizabeth? Something crashed to the ground behind her. Her heart raced. Unable to detect what had made the noise, she whirled around. She turned to go back into the lodge and crashed into hard muscle. She screamed.

She took a step back and looked up. "Gavin."

He gripped her forearms, steadying her. "What's going on? Where is Elizabeth? What are you doing out here alone?"

"Don't be mad at her. She just went inside…to…to find some photos." She turned sideways. A brick had fallen from the unfinished wall. That was the crashing noise she had heard. "We thought it would be better if we let you sleep."

He cupped a hand on her bare shoulder. "You're shaking. What happened?"

It was just so easy for her to fall back into a fearful place. She skirted past him. "Nothing, nothing."

He grabbed her arm. "Something is going on." He squared his shoulders, taking on that protective stance. "Did you hear something out here? Maybe I should check the perimeter."

"No, it was just my imagination." And that was the problem; the smallest thing triggered the memories of confinement. After two years of work with the counselor, she thought she was past this. She'd been lying to herself. Elijah would have a hold on her no matter what. He would be in her head forever.

He moved back toward her. "I can see you're upset. If there was no one out there, what is it?"

She couldn't bring herself to tell him. Here she had pushed so hard to be alone, to not feel as though she was under guard all the time, and it was obvious that she wasn't ready for that. She couldn't handle being alone. Normal would never happen.

Elizabeth emerged from a side room, holding a stack of photo albums. "What's going on?"

Julia's throat felt tight. They wouldn't understand. "You'll have to excuse me." She ran up the stairs into her room and slumped down on the floor. For the first time since the trial date had been set, she began to doubt if she could face Elijah. She'd been driven by a desire to find justice for Marlena, and now she wasn't sure she could do that. A sense of hopelessness filled her. Julia ran her hands through her short, red hair. She was dripping water everywhere.

She rose to her feet and grabbed a towel from the bath.

Someone rapped gently on the door. "Julia, it's Gavin. If you want to go back out in the pool, I'd be glad to sit out there with you."

She didn't want to face Gavin after all her talk about wanting to be free of the constant watch. "No, I think I'll—" She turned slightly and noticed the perfume on the dresser. As she walked over to it, her heart swelled with affection and her mood elevated. It was the perfume she had intended to buy at the department store. She picked up the bottle and swung the door open. "Did you...?"

"I asked Elizabeth to go into town and get it for you."

Overwhelmed with gratitude and forgetting that she was dripping wet, she reached up and hugged his neck. "Thank you." He *had* understood how much it meant to her.

At first, his arms wrapped around her waist and he welcomed the hug, but then he stepped back and lifted her arms off his shoulders. As he studied her, his Adam's apple moved up and down. "I know it's not quite the same thing as buying it yourself, but I thought maybe it would give you hope…about the future."

The tone of his voice was all business, and she knew she had made a mistake in gushing over the gift. His kindness had so moved her that once again, she had blundered. She hadn't read the signals he gave her clearly. "I'm glad that both you and Elizabeth did that for me." Her cheeks flushed, and she struggled to keep the hurt out of her voice.

"Are you sure you don't want to get back in the pool?" Gavin asked. "I would be happy to stand watch."

Of course—standing watch was his job. "No, I think I'll just study for a while and turn in early." The embarrassment she felt was so intense, she just needed to hide. She slipped back into the room and closed the door, then leaned against it, staring at the ceiling and taking in gulps of air. Though she resisted it, the tears rimmed again. She needed to do something to beat back the encroaching despair. She wasn't moving forward in her life. She couldn't be alone without Elijah getting into her head and paralyzing her. Gavin probably thought she acted like a teenager.

Julia spent several hours doing practice tests, and then she read a book she'd found in Elizabeth's library.

By the time she crawled into bed, it was after nine. She was bone weary and her leg still hurt a little.

She lay in bed staring at the ceiling. Outside her door, she heard Gavin scoot his chair across the floor. The embarrassment she felt over her impulsive hug made it hard to keep her voice neutral. "Good night, Gavin."

"Night. Big day tomorrow. We'll drive over to Billings for the trial prep with the lawyers."

"I know." She fought to keep her voice steady as apprehension invaded her thoughts. The plan to meet the lawyers at a larger hotel had been set up the minute a trial date was established, long before they had decided to move her to the hot springs. She squeezed her eyes shut. Could she even do this?

The next morning, Julia went through the motions of getting ready—putting on slacks and a blouse, applying makeup, yet all the time feeling numb. As if the only way she could face this was to pretend as though it wasn't happening. She'd had dreams the night before about seeing Elijah's sneering face in a crowd.

She gripped her chest where it felt tight and then took in a deep breath. She had to do this. She had to find the strength.

Help me, Lord.

She looked up at the auburn-headed woman in the mirror. Sunset red made her pale skin look even more porcelain. She darkened her eyeliner and intensified the brows. That was a little better. She picked up the perfume bottle and sprayed some on her wrists and behind her ears.

When she came down the stairs, Gavin was waiting for her at the bottom. He wore a T-shirt, leather jacket and khakis with the big pockets in the legs. He held up a plastic container. "Elizabeth made us some food for the road."

"That was nice of her." The photo albums Elizabeth had dug up rested on one of the couches in the lobby. They'd have to go through them another time.

He leaned toward her as concern washed over his face. "You doing okay?"

She nodded and managed a plastic smile. What a liar she was. She couldn't burden him even more, and she wasn't sure she was even ready to open up about the memories. She certainly wasn't ready to talk about stepping over a line with the hug. Gavin's job wasn't to be her emotional babysitter.

"I know you said you thought you were just hearing things, but I walked the grounds last night just to be sure."

Though she still felt anxious about leaving the springs, knowing that he was with her calmed her. "You just never go off duty, do you?"

"It's what I'm getting paid for."

Of course, his protectiveness of her wasn't because he had feelings for her. He was getting a paycheck. He was just a man who did his job and did it well. She had to keep reminding herself that.

"Let's go. Let's get this done."

NINE

Gavin escorted Julia outside. She'd taken his breath away when he had seen her at the top of the stairs. It was hard to keep his voice casual now. "Your leg seems a lot better. You're not limping as much."

"I suppose." She clipped her words.

No surprise that she was short with him. He'd hurt her feelings. It had taken all his strength to step free of her hug last night. Elizabeth had been right. No matter what the reason for giving a gift like perfume, women would always assume romantic intent. He'd hurt her. Sometimes he could be such a dumb clod.

Julia climbed into the SUV, and Gavin took the wheel. Would he be breaking his word to her father if he simply explained why he had pulled back? Maybe on some unconscious level, he'd wanted her to see the gift of perfume as a romantic overture. From the first time he had seen her, he had felt the smolder of attraction.

Neither one of them needed romantic complications in their lives right now. Julia had to get through this trial and on with her life. He needed to decide if he was even going to continue to be a bodyguard. He glanced over at her as she ran her fingers through her red hair. Would she have so much confidence in him if she knew his choices as a bodyguard had ended his friend's driving career in Florida?

There was something else going on with her, though; he'd seen it last night when she'd run out of the pool. She'd held it together when they were actually being chased, but then fell apart when she imagined noises. Maybe this was the frailty that her father had referenced.

As the car rolled down the road, he found himself wanting to help her work through whatever had upset her while she was in the hot springs. It probably had something to do with her time in captivity. "What was it like, in the cult?"

A look of shock defined her features, and for a moment, he feared he had been too blunt. She rubbed her fingers on her pant legs and took in a breath. "Elijah wanted me to stay in the house because he was afraid an outsider would see me and recognize me. People from town came sometimes to buy produce or deliver things." Her voice had a slight lilt to it. "Marlena found ways to keep me busy even though I was mostly inside. We would bake and work on quilts." She looked out the window and then back at him. "All the curtains were drawn. The windows were nailed shut. I craved sunshine.

"Even when Elijah was gone, there was always this tension in the air. Because you feared he would come back and..." She shook her head. "You never knew what would upset him, what would set him off."

As he listened, his throat went dry. Anger coursed through him for what she had endured, what had been done to her. He shook his head. "I'm so sorry."

"There were some good moments. Once in a while, when Elijah went to town, Marlena would sneak me out. The cult members grew really beautiful gardens with tall sunflowers." She stared at her hands as her voice wavered. "I loved looking at those sunflowers, the way they follow the sun. Something about that gave me hope."

Her resilience and her survival instinct never ceased to amaze him. "Last night, in the hot springs, something bothered you."

She turned her head away and stared out the window. "It's hard to explain. But Elijah's beliefs and lies were like snakes crawling around in my brain. He'd tell me things to upset me." She turned to look at him. "Once he told me my father was dead."

Gavin's breath hitched. "So it's like you still hear his voice sometimes."

She touched her finger to her head. "The past two years, I learned how to keep that voice from having power over me, but…"

He completed her thought. "But every once in a while, the voice gets in."

"Yes, exactly."

"So that's what last night was about." Gavin turned out on to the main road and hit his turn signal as he contemplated what she had told him.

"It'll be good to have this trial prep over and done with," she said.

The lawyers thought they could get the prep done in two days if they worked around the clock. Hopefully, Julia was strong enough to relive the events surrounding the murder that the trial prep would bring up. After last night, he had concerns. "Are you sure you feel ready for this?"

She spoke without hesitating. "I have to be ready."

He checked the rearview mirror.

Julia sighed. "Here we go again." Her comment was spoken lightheartedly.

"I'm sure we'll be fine." He hoped his expression was reassuring. The least he could do was make her feel physically safe, even if he couldn't stop what she would have to face emotionally with the trial prep.

The closer they got to Billings, the tighter the knot of tension in Julia's stomach became. She pulled her beads out of her purse, but could only stare at them.

Gavin veered the car over to an exit. When the tall towers of three hotels, clustered together in the distance, came into view, her anxiety shot through the roof.

Gavin glanced over at her. "You going to make it?"

Talking with him about the effect Elijah had on her, seeing how accepting he was, had only made her trust him more. She'd seen right from the start that he would do everything in his power to keep her physically safe, but now she knew she could share the details about her captivity, and he would understand.

Julia sat up straighter in her seat. "Thanks for worrying about me so much. I'm going to be okay."

Billings was two hundred miles from the town where the trial would take place in Thornburg. They weren't likely to run into followers. Arranging for the lawyers to come to the larger city would give them a degree of anonymity. In a small town, everyone knew when strangers showed up. They pulled into the parking lot, which was only half-full of cars.

"The lawyers are waiting in the conference room. I'll take you there and then get your stuff moved to your room. I need to get a sense of how this place is laid out. Before you're finished, I'll be right outside the conference-room door." He cupped his hand on her shoulder. "Okay?"

She managed a nod. There was a part of her that wanted to ask him to be in the conference room with her. Trial prep would be easier to face with him there. But that really went beyond his job description.

"You can do this, Julia?"

"I will do this." She sounded more confident than she felt. She pushed the door open and planted her feet on the ground.

Gavin walked behind her. He turned his head side to side, probably taking note of each make and model of the cars in the lot. Gavin held the door for her as they entered the lobby. There was no one behind the checkout counter.

An older man who had more age spots than hair sat on one of the lobby couches with his laptop open. "You folks here for the big orchid show?"

"No, we're just…sightseeing." As more people whirled through the lobby, Gavin placed a protective hand on the small of Julia's back. Fear had clamored to the surface as she searched the face of each person who passed by her, and he had tuned into her emotional state. The warmth of his hand sank through to her skin.

The old man clicked away on his computer. "You're lucky to get a room. All the hotels in town are full. If you get some time, you should head down to the main auditorium and have a look at the flowers."

"We'll try to work that into our schedule." Julia leaned a little closer to Gavin. The man had assumed they were husband and wife. She could play that role if it kept her safe. It didn't mean anything.

"I wonder where the help has gone?" Gavin bent his head toward the empty checkout counter. He glanced at a poster-size map of the hotel on the wall. "The conference room is just up the stairs on the third floor and around the corner. Maybe I should take you there and come back for the keys once you're safe with the lawyers."

Gavin led Julia down a hallway toward an elevator. They stood several feet apart while they waited for the elevator to open up. A man with a yellow briefcase came and stood by Julia.

Attraction flashed through his eyes as he assessed her head to toe. "Well, hello there."

The man had leered more than he had looked at her. She'd seen that gleam before in the eyes of the men at the cult. Gavin moved toward her and wrapped an arm around her waist as if to say "she's with me."

She appreciated the rescue. When they stepped on to the elevator, the man with the briefcase didn't follow them. As the doors closed, he leaned forward, studying Julia intently as his eyes grew wide.

Once the doors slid shut, Julia said, "Thanks, that guy was kind of creepy."

Gavin watched the numbers on the elevator panel. "No problem."

The door slid open, and they rounded the corner to where a man in a suit stood outside a conference-room door.

Julia quickened her pace. "That's him. That's Mr. Fleming."

The lawyer's eyes brightened as they approached. He held his hands up toward Julia and embraced her in a hug. "Julia, good to see you again."

A woman dressed in a simple navy suit emerged from the room. She held out a hand. "You must be Gavin Shane. I'm Victoria Fleming. Roy and I are partners in life and in the law firm." She turned toward Julia and offered her open arms. Victoria was more than just an expert on prosecuting cult members. It was her kindness that had gotten Julia through the depositions.

Gavin said, "Julia is not to leave this room for any reason until I am back here to get her. In fact, when I am on my way back, I'll give you a call and then knock three times. If I stand outside the door and wait, I'll call too much attention to this room."

"We know what we're up against." Roy tugged on his suit jacket. "I'm sure Julia is going to need a break, but we're going to get through as much of this as we can."

Gavin nodded. The lawyers ushered Julia into the room. Tension squeezed Gavin's chest as the door closed. He'd feel better when he could be in the room with her, but it would be dereliction of duty not to walk the hotel and get familiar with the layout.

It took him twenty minutes to put Julia's overnight bag in her room and to check into the room next to hers. The hotel had alarms on all the outside doors. After eleven o'clock, people without card keys could only come and go by the front entrance. He checked both parking lots for anything out of the ordinary. When he came back inside, the man with the yellow briefcase passed him in the lobby.

Gavin had wanted to pound the guy into the ground when he'd so overtly come on to Julia at the elevator. The flush in her cheeks and her obvious embarrassment was a reminder of her inexperience in dealing with men.

As he moved through the lobby, Gavin felt the weight of the man's gaze on his back. He headed up the stairs. He went up a few steps then turned so he could survey the lobby, feigning nonchalance. The man was gone.

Gavin took the stairs to the third floor, phoning the Flemings on the way up. He knocked on the door three times, then a lock clicked and the door opened.

Julia sat in a chair pushed away from the conference table. She held a string of beads in her lap. Her expression warmed when he entered the room.

Victoria leaned close to Gavin and whispered, "Julia has the answers to our questions down pat. Now we're taking her through the mock cross. We go through possible lines of questioning the defense might use."

Roy paced in front of Julia. The friendly demeanor Gavin had picked up on earlier was gone. Roy's posture was stiff, his chin tilted. He had taken on the role of the no-holds-barred defense attorney.

"So." Roy stopped his pacing and leaned toward Julia. "You said at first all the doors were locked, but later Elijah would leave them open. In fact, the previous witness has testified that he heard a conversation between you and Mr. True in which he told you you could leave the compound. Is that correct?"

Julia clutched the beads in her hand. "You don't understand."

Roy shot back. "Answer the question."

"Yes, that is what Elijah said, but he didn't mean it. It was a game he played. Sometimes the doors were locked and sometimes they weren't."

"So you are saying you didn't want to leave? Maybe you had started to like it there? After all, you stayed for seven years."

"No, don't you understand? Elijah didn't have to lock the doors after a while because the locks were inside my head. I knew if I tried to run, he'd catch me and put me in that dark place." Her hand trembled as she brought it up to her face. "Even if I got into town, there were cult members who lived there who would tell Elijah." Julia drew in a ragged breath. "I started to believe that there was no place I could go where he wouldn't find me."

Gavin lurched out of his seat, but Victoria stopped him.

Victoria piped up, "Julia, we're sorry to have to put you through this. You know they will do everything to make it look as though you aren't a reliable witness because of your psychological state. Are you prepared for that?"

"I know," Julia said resolutely.

"If this line of questioning went on too long at some point, we would object on the grounds that it's immaterial to the murder. But it is important that the jury sees that you can hold up to the badgering, and it works in our favor because it reveals to the jury what a monster Elijah could be."

Julia pulled a purple bead from the bag and put it on the wire.

Roy's posture softened. "You holding up okay?"

Julia straightened in her chair. "I know that we have to do this. I want Elijah put away." Her lower lip quivered.

Victoria flipped through a pile of papers. "Let's move on to your testimony about the murder. That's where they are really going to start to tear you apart. Just stick to the story you gave in the deposition."

Standing to one side of Julia, Roy resumed his arrogant posture, lacing his fingers together behind his back. "Let's move on to the night of the murder."

Julia cast a glance toward Gavin. The look on her face made him want to rush over to her and take her in his arms.

"So, you said you heard Marlena Kenyon and Elijah arguing."

"Yes."

"What were they arguing about?"

"Elijah told Marlena that it was time he chose a husband for me, but that is not really what the argument was about. Any time he got worked up, he brought up the marriage thing. Earlier that day, one of the cult members in town said he saw guys who looked like FBI. Elijah was paranoid about being arrested. He was tense and angry all that day. When he got that way, he wanted to control everyone and everything."

"So you heard them arguing, but you didn't witness the actual murder?"

Julia's eyes lost focus for a moment, but she recovered. "I'd been sent to my room. I heard it. It had to be Elijah. There was no one else in the house."

Roy tapped his finger on his chin. "So you didn't actually see him strike her."

"I heard the fight. He locked me in the room. I knew how to jimmy the lock…but—but I couldn't get out there fast enough. When I came out, I saw Elijah holding the hammer…and—Marlena on the floor."

Roy leaned toward Julia until he was invading her space. "What was your relationship with Marlena Kenyon?"

"She was my friend. She was like a mom to me." Julia looked directly at Roy and spoke with confidence.

"So are you saying that the previous witness has lied? He said that you wanted Marlena out of the way. That, in fact, you wanted to be Elijah's wife. Weren't all the other women married by the time they were sixteen? You wanted Elijah. That is why your marriage to another man was delayed."

Julia spoke rapidly without taking a breath. "No, that's not true. I wasn't jealous of her. Marlena was my friend. Marlena protected me. She didn't want me to go through what she had been through."

"Marlena was your friend and yet, on the night she died, you ran away. Was she still breathing when you got out of there?"

"No…I mean, I didn't touch her, but I could see she was dead." She opened her mouth as if to say more, but could only shake her head.

Gavin's arm muscles tensed. Julia seemed to be unraveling before his eyes. Victoria patted his arm, indicating that he needed to stay put. He summoned every ounce of strength he had not to rush over to her.

Julia forged ahead. "Elijah ran out of the house, and I heard him telling everyone that I had killed her. I…I…I wanted to help her. I couldn't get the door unlocked fast enough…" As though she were trying to find the strength to continue, Julia bent her head so her hair fell over her face.

Gavin's hands curled into fists. How long did they have to put her through this?

Roy hovered over her. "You say that Elijah was the only one in the house, so it had to be him, but there was another person in the house that night."

Julia lifted her head. A fierceness entered her eyes. "I would never do anything to hurt Marlena. I'm not the one on trial."

"Yet you ran away as fast as you could."

Gavin rose from his chair. "Maybe we should stop now."

"We have to do this, Gavin." Julia's voice was paper thin as she stared at the carpet.

"I'm with Gavin. I think we need a break." Victoria pushed file folders to one side.

Roy offered Julia a sideways hug when she got out of her chair and whispered a reassurance in her ear. "Let's break for a couple of hours. I'm sure Julia would like to get something to eat."

Gavin strode over to Julia. "Come on," he spoke gently. "Let's go get some air."

Once outside the room, Julia placed her hand on the wall. She was really shaken up. "That was harder than I thought it was going to be. My legs are wobbly."

"I'll help you get to the hotel room." Gavin wrapped his arms around her narrow waist. "This helps with the cover that we're husband and wife." He tried to keep his tone light.

Julia bent her head. In this light, her red hair took on a coppery tone.

"I didn't like watching that," Gavin said. Seeing her ripped to pieces by the questioning tore at his insides.

She leaned against him as they walked. "I need to be prepared, or it will just be worse when Elijah's lawyers get me on the stand."

"I know." It was still hard to see her raked over the coals, even if it was for a good reason.

She slowed her pace. "Do *you* think there was something more I could have done?"

"What do you mean?"

She stopped, pulled free of his grasp and turned to face him. She looked up at him as her eyes glazed. "To save Marlena. All those questions make me play that night over and over in my mind. Maybe if I had done something different. Maybe if I hadn't let Elijah lock me in the room in the first place."

Now that he had a greater understanding of all that she had been through, he wished he could lift the anguish from her and carry it himself. "Don't play the maybe game. You have no reason to feel guilty. You did everything you knew to do at the time." He touched his palm to her cheek.

"I want to believe that." She collapsed into his arms, nestling her face against his chest. He held her. Several people passed by them on the balcony outside her room. He could hear the sound of people splashing in the pool several floors below.

Standing out in the open like this made them vulnerable. He waited for her to recover before suggesting that they go into the hotel room.

They ate a meal ordered from room service. Then while Julia napped, Gavin paced to keep his energy up. He splashed water on his face and made a cup of coffee. Julia slept curled up on the covers, her red hair falling over her face.

By the time he finished his coffee, Julia was awake and ready to go.

He phoned the Flemings to let them know they were ready to get started. He closed his phone and addressed her. "They'll be at the conference room in ten minutes."

As they left the room, Gavin fell in behind Julia. They were getting used to walking in tandem. Julia seemed less bothered by his proximity.

The floor where the conference room was was empty. Gavin checked his watch; it was the dinner hour for most people.

"Quiet up here," said Julia.

"It certainly is." A voice behind them caused both of them to pivot.

Gavin gripped Julia's arm above the elbow, prepared to whisk her away or push her to the floor and cover her if he needed to.

The man with the yellow briefcase stood behind them.

Gavin planted his feet shoulder width apart. The gun in his holster pressed against his ribs. "Who are you?"

"Relax, man. I'm a reporter with the *Montana Tribune.*"

Gavin's hands curled into fists. Like knowing he was dealing with the press was supposed to make him relax.

"The red hair is a nice touch, but that angelic face with the big blue eyes is hard to forget. Her face was everywhere two years ago." The reporter took a step toward Julia. "I'd just like to ask Ms. Randel a few questions."

Gavin stepped between Julia and the man. "She's not answering questions. You're not going to do a story on her."

"It's a little late for that. She's already in the evening edition that came out an hour ago. Julia Randel is news. I would like to do a follow-up story and get her perspective on the upcoming trial."

"I'm not talking to anyone." Julia's voice sounded forceful, strong.

"Please go." Gavin narrowed his eyes and took on a stance that told the man there was no room for negotiation.

The man held his hands up, palms out. "Fine. I

offered. She could have given me her take on all this."
He walked backwards toward the stairs.

Gavin waited until the man slipped out of view before
glancing around for a newspaper dispenser. He put in
three quarters and pulled out the evening edition.

Julia had moved to the conference-room door.

He flipped through the newspaper. At least she wasn't
front-page news.

"The door is still locked." She spoke louder to be
heard across the empty floor. "The Flemings must have
been delayed."

Gavin made his way across the carpet, still scanning
the newspaper. Her story was on page eight, along with
a photograph of him and Julia standing outside her hotel
room. The quality of the picture indicated it had been
taken with a telephoto lens. The article itself speculated
why two high-powered lawyers who specialized in prosecuting cult members were at the same hotel as Julia
Randel. The rest of the article was a recap of the events
that had led up to the trial—Julia's captivity, escape and
the filing of murder and kidnapping charges against
Elijah.

Gavin gritted his teeth. It was enough damage. The
Tribune was a big newspaper with statewide distribu-
tion. The cult members would get wind of it, if they
hadn't already. Now he was mad. They couldn't stay
in the hotel. They were going to have to change venues
to finish the trial prep. The hot springs were still safe,
but if someone followed the Flemings as they came and
went, that sanctuary would be comprised. They'd have
to find a whole new place—not an easy task with the
trial only weeks away.

A group of people shuffled through the open area
outside the conference rooms. Gavin looked up as the

people cleared away. His heart stopped. The area outside the door where Julia had been standing a second ago was empty.

TEN

Still stirred up about the news story, Julia turned her attention to her purse to pull out her beads. A group of people walked by, blocking her view of Gavin. Movement erupted from behind a nearby coat rack. Terror spread through Julia as two men lurched toward her.

One shoved a gun into her side. "Any noise and you're dead."

Her purse fell to the ground, but she managed to hold on to the bag of beads and conceal them in her fist. The men steered her away from the people, around a corner to a service elevator.

Gripping her forearm, one of the men pushed the elevator button and waited. The gun still pressed into her ribs. With her hands behind her, she allowed a few beads to fall to the carpet.

The elevator doors opened. They pushed her inside and shoved a pillowcase over her head. Her heart pounded erratically. Fabric pressed against her mouth as she struggled for breath.

One of the men pressed his fingernails into her arm. She could smell him, a blend of dirt and sweat that repulsed her. The elevator came to a stop, and she was pushed forward. The floor beneath was smooth. Even through the pillowcase, the air felt thicker down here, more humid. They must be close to a laundry room or kitchen. Her hand gripped the bag of beads.

"Let's get this done quickly. Elijah said no hesitation." The gravelly voice sent chills through Julia.

She waited for the moment when the men's footsteps and voices drowned out other sounds before dropping two more beads. Would it be enough to let Gavin know what direction they had taken her?

Gavin felt as though he had been punched in the stomach.

The Flemings, who had just emerged from the stairwell, must have read the panic on his face.

Victoria raced to his side. "What is it?"

"Call security now." He didn't have time to wait for hotel cops to show up. The followers weren't going to toy with them or try to negotiate. They were going to kill Julia. All they needed was the right location. He had ten minutes tops before Julia would lose her life.

Roy had already taken out his phone.

Gavin ran over to the last place he had seen Julia standing. He scanned the area. "What floor did you guys come from?"

"The fifth floor." Victoria massaged her temples and shook her head. "This is terrible."

That meant they hadn't taken the stairwell going up. The Flemings would have spotted them. His gaze darted around the open area. The elevator was across from the conference-room door. He would have spotted the followers if they had taken her that way. Gavin stepped toward the coat rack. Julia's purse lay open on the carpet, and a service elevator was just beyond that.

Something by the elevator caught his eye. He ran over and picked it up. A single glass bead.

Thank you, Julia.

Her ability to think fast under pressure never ceased to amaze him.

Victoria came around the coat rack. "Roy is going to stay until security comes. Can I help?"

"Come with me. Two can search faster than one." He pushed the button on the service elevator and stepped inside. Victoria followed behind him. He studied the panel for a moment. "We've got two floors below us and a basement."

Unless they had taken her to one of the hotel rooms, the basement would be the most secluded. "You get off on the second floor. She left a trail for us. Look for one of these." He held up the purple glass bead. "Don't do anything if you find one; just call me."

Victoria nodded. "Got it. I know what these men are capable of."

Gavin steadied himself and shook off the rising anxiety that would make it impossible to work. He had to focus on finding her. He couldn't allow the images of what might be happening to her to take hold. Though it felt strange, he stuttered through a prayer asking God to help him find her.

Victoria got off on the second floor. Gavin rode the elevator to the basement. When he stepped off, the air became more humid and smelled of bleach. He drew his weapon and pressed against the wall. He walked past a room filled with whirring washing machines, dryers and piles of linens.

He peeked around the door frame and did a quick scan; no one was in the room.

There was a door off to the side. He heard voices

whispering. Gavin slipped into the laundry room. The voices were barely audible above the tumbling of sheets in the dryer.

He made his way over to the door.

Sweat trickled down Julia's back. The room was steamy, like a sauna. A smell hung in the air that she couldn't quite identify. Was it bleach or some kind of cleaner? Chlorine?

They had tied her hands behind her back and made her kneel on the floor. With the hood still on, she couldn't see anything. She could only hear the cult members' footsteps pounding around her as they argued.

"Just do it now." One of the followers spat out the words. The rage in his voice made her shudder.

"This is a bad idea. I say we take her out of here," said the other.

Julia curled her bound hands into fists. She had long since run out of beads and had let the plastic bag fall silently to the carpet before they had dragged her in here and tied her up.

"Too late for that. That bodyguard of hers probably alerted security. The building is in lockdown by now. We're out of options. Let's just do this."

Julia heard the slide on a handgun ratchet back. She froze, unable to take a breath. Beneath the pillow case, she squeezed her eyes shut.

This is it, God.

"They'll hear the gunshots."

"So what if they catch us? This is for Elijah."

Footsteps shuffled.

A flash of memory, of Gavin reaching his hand up to touch her cheek and his words, "I'll keep you safe," sparked inside her mind as she felt the cold barrel of the handgun press against her temple.

The door burst open suddenly.

"Hey, what are you doing in here?" The scream from the follower was bloodcurdling.

Gavin raised his weapon and kicked open the door.

Two men sitting at a table engaged in a card game screamed, jumped up from their chairs and stumbled backwards.

One of them held up his hands. "We're on our break, honest."

"Sorry." Gavin dropped the gun by his side. "I was looking for somebody else." His cell phone rang.

Victoria's voice sounded frantic. "I found beads on the first floor by the pool."

Gavin holstered his gun and ran toward the door. "They must have her in one of those rooms by the pool."

"I see another bead." Victoria was out of breath from running.

Gavin was halfway up the stairs. "Victoria, no, don't follow the trail. Wait for me."

He had pushed open the stairwell door when he heard gunshots. Gavin raced across the expanse toward the source of the gunshots. People crawled out of the pool, running toward the safety of their rooms. Only one man, wearing an orange shirt, remained on the side of the pool where the gunshots had come from.

Please, dear God, let her be okay.

Victoria came around the corner. Her face had gone completely white. "This way." Her voice trembled from shock.

Gavin ran toward the room that housed the pool

maintenance equipment. A man, dressed in janitor's coveralls, lay on the floor bleeding, but still alive. Another man, his eyes wild with fear, held up his hands and backed up to a wall.

Gavin stomped toward the man with his hands up. "Where is she?"

"He—he." The man gulped. He had the long hair and beard characteristic of cult members.

Gavin grabbed the man's shirt collar. "Where is she?"

The man pointed a shaking finger. "He took her to the parking lot."

Gavin turned back toward Victoria. "Make sure the police know what happened here." He pointed toward the man on the floor. "Get this man some medical attention. I have to find Julia."

Gavin's heart pounded as he ran toward the back door and pushed it open. He scanned the parking lot. A car started up in a far corner. Then he detected movement in his peripheral vision.

Julia's red hair flashed. Judging from her bent posture, the cult member either had a gun pressed into the small of her back or her hands were tied behind her.

Gavin eased in behind a van, crouching slightly. They were headed toward a small vehicle parked off by itself. Shielding himself behind cars, Gavin worked his way toward them with his weapon drawn. Ten yards stretched between the last car that hid him from view and Julia and her kidnapper. Gavin waited for the moment when the man's guard would be down. He'd have to let go of Julia to pull his keys out. The man put his gun in his waistband and reached into his pocket.

Feet pounded pavement. Gavin closed the distance between them, whacking the man on the back of the head before he had a change to turn around. The man crumpled on to the asphalt with a moan.

Gavin pulled out his pocketknife and cut the rope that bound Julia's wrists. "I'm sure the police will want a statement from us, and then we have to go."

Julia's breath came in short gasps. "Thank you. I thought I was…"

Gavin glanced at an orange compact car as a realization exploded in his brain. The man in the orange shirt was the same man in the ill-fitting suit who'd been in the department store. There were more followers in that hotel. The newspaper article had made them crawl out of the woodwork. He couldn't risk staying in this town one moment longer.

"On second thought, let's get you out of here. I'll have to straighten things out with the police later."

He ushered Julia through the lot toward his vehicle.

"I'm with you. Let's go." Despite the trauma of the last ten minutes, her voice sounded resolute and strong.

They got into the SUV.

Gavin handed her his phone. "Call Roy and Victoria. Let them know about the man in the parking lot so the police can pick him up. Tell them why we can't stick around. They'll know how to handle the police."

"Where are we going?"

Gavin's mind raced. "Just make that first call. I need to come up with a plan." The hot springs wasn't compromised. He needed to get Julia back there safe, but he needed to make sure they weren't followed.

Julia finished the phone call with Roy. "Now what?"

"I need you to call Elizabeth. Have her borrow a friend's car. Ask her to come up with a location that is secluded and away from the hot springs, someplace where it would be easy to know you were being followed."

"What are you going to do?"

"They know this vehicle. They'll follow it if they see it. You're going to go back to the hot springs with Elizabeth, and I'm going to lead them away from the hot springs and make arrangements to get a different car."

"No, I want to stay with you." It was the first time he'd heard fear in her voice since rescuing her. The adrenaline was probably masking a lot of the shock. In a little while, she'd hit a wall and the reality of what had happened could overwhelm her. He needed to stay with her at least that long.

"Let's just drive for a while." He saw the risk in the plan, too. The thought of trusting her to anyone else made his chest ache. "Make the call to Elizabeth. Tell her we need a couple hours before we can get there."

She drew the phone to her ear. As he listened to Julia talk, he could hear the shock over all that had happened emerge in her voice. She stuttered. Her voice grew weak, and when he looked over at her, the phone was shaking in her hands.

He longed to take her in his arms and hold her until the fear subsided, but stopping would be dangerous.

Julia grabbed a piece of paper and a pen and wrote down directions as Elizabeth gave them. She hung up the phone. Julia read the directions out loud to him and then added, "It's an old dirt logging-road, single lane, and it dead ends. It'll be dark by the time we get there, so we'll see headlights if we are being followed. She'll be waiting for us."

"Perfect, that should work. I'm going try to make arrangements to ditch this car. So we eliminate one of the factors that make us easy to find." He glanced over at her. "Listen, I'm sorry about what happened back there. I got too worked up over the newspaper article. There shouldn't have been that kind of distance between us." He was angry at himself for his moment of inattention.

"It wasn't your fault. They would have found an opportunity one way or another." She couldn't blame him. He had saved her life, and now he was talking about separating.

Julia swallowed to push down the rising anxiety over the idea of being apart from Gavin. She wrapped the blazer she'd been wearing tighter around her. Her clothes, including her winter coat, were back at the hotel. "Why can't we just go back to the hot springs together?" She forced the words out, hoping Gavin didn't pick up on how unraveled she was. She needed to stay strong.

"We seem to be spending a lot of time in this car, don't we?" His voice had a gentle quality, but he had avoided answering her question.

She appreciated his attempt to talk her away from the emotional ledge she was on with his comforting tone. Her throat tightened. She wasn't going to cry. "Yeah, we spend a lot of time...running." Even as she bit her lower lip, warm liquid filled her eyes. The car was dark; he wouldn't see.

Gavin glanced in the rearview mirror.

Julia sat up straighter as panic erupted anew. "They're following us again, aren't they?"

"I don't know. That car didn't pass when I slowed down. It could be nothing." The headlights of the SUV created cones of illumination on the dark country road.

"There's the turnoff." No matter what she did, she couldn't force down that awful feeling that her life was like a piece of glass bent and stressed to the breaking point. The trial prep had caused doubts to creep in. Maybe she wasn't strong enough to face Elijah.

Gavin hit the blinker and slowed. The washboard terrain of the dirt road made the car bounce. Julia looked behind her. No headlights. They wouldn't be followed here.

Ten minutes later, Elizabeth's car came into view. Tiny flakes of snow, driven sideways by the wind, swirled through the headlights. Elizabeth opened the car door and stood beside it. The white down coat made her stand out against the darkness that surrounded her.

Gavin stopped the car, but kept the engine running. Before Julia was even out of the car, he was behind her. Elizabeth came up to them, and Gavin addressed her. "Stay here for at least a half hour, off the road, out of sight with the lights out. I don't know what cell reception is like, but I will try to call you to let you know they took the bait and are following me."

Elizabeth nodded. "When will you be back?"

"I don't know. This might take a while."

Julia shivered from the cold. Gavin turned to go. Julia stepped toward him, wrapped her arms around his neck and hugged him. "Be safe."

This time he didn't pull free of her hug. He melted against her. "That's my job." He touched her hair with his palm.

What he was doing was risky. The followers thought she was in the SUV. If they caught up with him, they would probably kill him. She hugged him tighter before letting go.

Elizabeth tugged on Julia's sleeve. "Come on, you'll catch your death standing out here without a coat."

Julia watched as Gavin strode back to his car, got in and turned around. The glaring red of the taillights burned her eyes. Would she see him again?

Elizabeth led Julia back to the car. They waited an hour, then drove home on the dark, silent road. No other cars passed them or followed them.

Once they were at the hot springs, Elizabeth said, "Maybe tonight it would be better if you slept in my house. You can have my bed and I'll sleep on the couch. We'll be all right. I have a shotgun, and I know how to use it."

Julia didn't argue. Her body and mind seemed to be responding to all the trauma and worry by going numb. "I don't even have a toothbrush. All my stuff got left at the hotel."

"That problem is easily solved. I always have extras that guests can purchase." Elizabeth showed Julia the room and then said, "I'll leave you alone now, but I'll just be right outside if you need anything."

After Elizabeth closed the door, Julia sat on the end of the bed staring at a cross-stitched picture of a child with her hands folded in prayer. As a little girl, her father had prayed with her every night.

Her faith had been a sort of shield from Elijah's twisted theology. It had carried her through a great deal. The trial prep and nearly being killed had robbed all the hope she had for the future.

She stared at the picture until it became unfocused. She lay down on top of the covers, pulling her legs up toward her stomach. Disillusionment seemed to come at her from all sides. Her faith felt fragile, and she wasn't sure if she had the strength to face Elijah.

She drifted off to sleep thinking of Gavin. Was he okay? She woke up several times in the night hearing noises. Each time, it took her half an hour to fall back to sleep.

The smell of bacon and coffee and the warmth of the winter sun streaming through her window awoke her for the final time. She stumbled into the kitchen where Elizabeth had prepared breakfast.

The living room and dining room of the cabin blended together into one room separated only by a counter with stools. Elizabeth stood in the small kitchen placing bacon on a paper towel.

"Did you raise all your children in this tiny house?"

"No, we had a house in town and a caretaker lived here. When Brian died and the kids all left, I decided to sell the big house and just live out here."

Elizabeth had brought the photo albums from the lodge and put them on the floor beside the couch.

Julia wrapped the sweater Elizabeth had loaned her tighter around her torso. Her stomach was doing somersaults. "Did...is Gavin back?"

Elizabeth shook her head.

The clock on the stove read 7:32 a.m. It had been at least twelve hours since they'd said good-bye. Julia struggled to not give into that sinking feeling of despair.

"I'm sure he'll be here soon." Elizabeth's attempt to sound positive fell flat.

"I hope so." Even as she spoke, tension knotted at the back of her neck.

Elizabeth forced a smile. "If you'll take a seat, I'll have breakfast ready for you in no time."

Julia looked around and saw no table to sit at, only a

counter and the couch where Elizabeth had folded her blankets and set them to one side.

"Feel free to sit on the sofa. It's more comfortable than the stools," Elizabeth said.

Julia sank into the plush couch.

"I brought those photo albums we intended to look at days ago when I went to get your toothbrush and toiletries." Elizabeth put two pieces of bread in the toaster.

Julia picked up the first album and opened it. Her father didn't keep many pictures of her mother on display, probably because it hurt too much to look at them. The first picture was of a much younger Elizabeth sitting on a horse. "You look so pretty."

After handing her a plate of bacon and scrambled eggs with toast, Elizabeth sat beside her. "Flip through about three pages."

Feeling a mixture of excitement and trepidation, Julia slowly lifted each page.

"There, that one is of Hannah, your mother."

The photograph was of a young, slender woman in a rowboat. Her curly, blond hair was blown back by the wind, and there was a look of exuberance on her face. A faint smile crossed Julia's lips as her heartbeat quickened. Her mother would have been about her age in that photograph. "She looks happy."

Her mother had tried to take her to parks and swimming pools, but there had always been a cloud hanging over what was intended to be a good time because the cancer had made her so tired.

Elizabeth pointed out several other photos. All of them were of a young woman who was vibrant and alive. Julia felt as though a hole in her heart had been mended. The pictures in her mind, which she had culled from sparse memories, were replaced by something more positive.

Elizabeth pointed out a photograph of her mom as a teenager running through a sprinkler. The summer sun created a rainbow in the arc of water. The image communicated sheer joy. A memory long buried floated back into Julia's head. The sound of her mother's laughter was as clear as if she was in the room.

Elizabeth pressed close to Julia. "What are you thinking about?"

"My mom couldn't do a lot of stuff, but she loved to read to me. We would sit in the big chair in the living room." Julia smiled. "I liked funny stories. She read them to me, and we would laugh until our bellies hurt." The memory of the scent of wisteria that surrounded her mother and the softness of her sweater as she nestled her little-girl head against it rose to the surface.

Elizabeth rubbed Julia back. "Hmmm…that is a good memory."

For the first time, Julia didn't bristle at Elizabeth's touch. She flipped the photo album to the next page.

Two men dressed in tuxedos stood with Elizabeth and Hannah, who were wearing flowing gowns.

"Prom." Julia traced the outline of the photograph with her finger as a familiar ache returned. "Did you have fun that night?"

"My date was more interested in dancing with someone else," Elizabeth mused.

"Such pretty dresses." Julia struggled to stay in the lightness of the moment. She couldn't focus on the loss of her own adolescence. Hope lay in looking toward the promise of the future.

Elizabeth wrapped an arm around Julia and pulled

her close. "Maybe the first pretty dress you get to wear will be your wedding gown."

Julia closed her eyes and snuggled into the hug. "I hadn't thought of that." God mends and restores in unexpected ways. Looking at the photographs had healed the wound from a long-ago loss. Maybe marriage would happen. All of that was so far off in the distance.

Elizabeth's grandfather clock struck eight. Julia pulled free of the hug as anxiety coiled in her stomach. Gavin should have been back by now. She rose to her feet and looked out the small window, unable to shake the feeling that something had happened to him.

ELEVEN

Gavin pulled into the lot outside the hot springs. The older-model Mustang he had borrowed from his high-school buddy Brandon ran like a dream. He had been followed for nearly fifty miles before he could shake the cult members. After that, he had contacted Brandon, who he knew ran a used-car lot in the area. The trade was temporary, but at least now he had minimized one of the factors that would compromise the security of the hot springs the next time they had to go out in public.

He pushed open the car door and stepped out into the cold morning. He found himself looking forward to seeing Julia again. It had been a risk to separate from her, and concern for her safety had crossed his mind more than once.

He opened the door to the lodge and stepped inside. "Hello, I'm back." The stillness of the place and the fact that the door had been unlocked alarmed him. "Julia?" He stepped toward the staircase as unease spread through him.

He ran over to the sliding glass doors and peered out. No sign of Elizabeth. No sign of Julia. He would never forgive himself if she had fallen back into the cult's hands. His anxiety clicked into high gear as he whirled around.

Julia stood in the doorway. "I heard you pull up. I assume that Mustang is your replacement car."

He breathed a sigh of relief. Her voice was like music to his ears. She must have come around to the front of the lodge and stepped through the open door. She held her hands together over her stomach. His breath caught in his throat. Even with his bad haircut and the unnatural shade of red, her beauty shone through.

"My new car. You like it?" He struggled to sound casual. The emotion that welled up inside him took him by surprise. Something had changed about her in the hours they had been apart. The vulnerability he saw in her wide blue eyes was still there, but she seemed peaceful.

"Pretty fancy." She stepped into the lodge and closed the door behind her. "How did you acquire something like that on such short notice?"

"You've got to know people. I have a friend from high school who owns a car lot in Highsdale, about sixty miles from here." Beneath the small talk, strong attraction stirred. When she had stood in the doorway, he'd had wanted to rush over to her.

"You grew up around here?"

"No, I grew up on the highline in northern Montana. I knew my friend had moved to this area."

She stepped toward him. "I really don't know much about you." Her eyes searched his. "I know our relationship is professional, that my father is paying you, but I wish I knew more."

"Not much to tell." He could talk about his childhood, but sharing too much might lead her to ask about Florida again. At first, he hadn't wanted to share about what had happened with Joshua because he was afraid it would shake her confidence in him as a bodyguard. But now, as he realized he was falling for her, he feared she would think less of him as a man if she knew.

She advanced toward him. "Everyone has stories to tell about their life."

He really wasn't ready to share his story yet. "I was worried about you when you didn't answer and that door was open." His voice was thick with emotion. Their time apart made him realize what a void he felt when he wasn't around her.

Her face flushed with color, and he wondered if she was feeling the same heated energy. "Elizabeth thought it would be safer to stay in her cabin."

The whole time they were apart, his thoughts returned to her over and over. On a job when another guard took a shift, it was normal to think about your client, to wonder about their safety. He had been in close quarters with clients for weeks on end before. But this time apart had been different. Not being around her had made him feel somehow incomplete. He really wanted to close the distance between them, to gather her in his arms and breathe in the scent of her hair and skin. He craved it.

"That was a good call on Elizabeth's part," he said, managing to sound casual.

"I know we both had our doubts about Elizabeth. But I do think she's looking out for us." She reached out and touched his arm as concern colored her voice. "You must be exhausted. You've been up all night."

The mention of sleep made his limbs feel heavy. "I suppose I should get in a couple hours' rest." As tired as he was, he didn't want to leave Julia's side.

"Please go and get some sleep."

"You sure?" The more he talked about rest, the sleepier he became. He was ready to crumple on the floor.

"Elizabeth and I will be okay," she assured him. "We'll stay inside. And she told me she has a shotgun and knows how to use it."

He made his way over to his room on the first floor, took a quick shower and collapsed into bed. What was it about Julia that was getting to him?

He rolled over as the fog of sleep invaded his thoughts. After seeing how she handled the kidnapping in the hotel and everything else, he could see that Julia was not the fragile creature William Randel had described. As he drifted off to sleep, he regretted making the promise to Julia's father.

He didn't view her as just another client anymore.

He slept for a long time and awoke to silence. He splashed water on his face and headed downstairs. The front door was closed, but still unlocked. Irritated, he turned the lock. When were they going to start paying attention to these things?

No one was in the outdoor pool. At least they had kept their word on that. The daytime sky was already starting to darken. This time of year, sunset happened around five o'clock. The dining room and the kitchen were both empty.

He quickened his pace as he made his way through the kitchen exit to the building with the hot tubs. He pushed open the door. The sound of women laughing and music playing allowed him to relax, but it bothered him that none of the doors had been locked.

Dressed in an oversize denim shirt with a scarf over her hair, Julia stood in one of the empty hot tubs scrubbing it, while Elizabeth mopped the tile floor.

"What is going on here?"

Elizabeth walked over to a CD player and turned down the volume.

Julia wrung out a sponge. "Since being outside isn't such a good idea, Elizabeth thought maybe we could get the indoor hot tubs going."

"Once we get this running, you can join us." Elizabeth moved toward a table where she had set an open can of soda. "It's going to take a while to get things shaped up, but it might be kind of fun. I'll fill the tub tonight."

Something in the way Julia and Elizabeth were relating to each other was different, more cordial. He smiled. "I appreciate the invite, but I really can't soak in a hot tub while I'm on duty."

Julia's shoulders slumped. "I wish you could join us. You work so hard."

"It seems like you should get a break once in a while," Elizabeth added. "We'll all go stir crazy if we just stay inside and do nothing."

"That's not how this job works. I'm going to walk the grounds and make sure everything is all clear." He turned toward Elizabeth and added, "You left the door to this place unlocked, by the way, along with the other doors."

Elizabeth grabbed a scrub brush off the table. "Sorry, I guess I forgot."

A little irritation tickled his nerves. She was so casual about the whole thing. He had thought they were on the same page with security. "It's bad enough you don't have an alarm system. You could at least take the standard precautions." He stalked toward the door. "You'll have to excuse me."

He had gotten back to the outdoor pool when

Elizabeth's voice hit his back. "Look, I didn't mean to sound so dismissive about the doors."

He wheeled back around. "It's basic security."

"I have lived here most of my life and never had to lock my doors. It's just habit. I don't think like you do. It doesn't mean I'm not concerned for Julia's safety. I'm not a security expert. I'm not constantly trying to predict ways that someone could get at Julia."

"What are you thinking about?"

"I'm thinking about what Julia needs emotionally," Elizabeth said.

They were both on the same side. They wanted what was best for Julia. Why were they always butting heads? "I know that, but the doors still need to be locked."

Elizabeth stepped closer to Gavin. Her expression grew serious. "Getting Julia to this trial isn't just about getting her physical body into that courtroom. When you were away, I saw how fond she's becoming of you, and I'm worried that it's not healthy."

Her comment took him aback. A level of attachment to a bodyguard was normal, but he would never do anything that would hinder Julia's recovery. "I understand that, and I'm not saying that she's undamaged by what she has been through, but Julia has more emotional stability than anyone is giving her credit for. She's not a child. I'm sure she resents everyone treating her like one. She's a strong, grown woman."

"Please stop fighting about me." Julia stood behind Elizabeth. She folded her arms over her chest to block out the cold. "Locking the door was as much my responsibility as Elizabeth's."

Had she heard the whole conversation? Sympathy flooded through him. Once again, in the name of protecting Julia, they were trying to run her life. He walked toward her. "Julia, you're shivering."

"I'm fine." She looked at Elizabeth and then at Gavin. "I care about both of you. Please don't fight about me and what I need." Her unwavering voice was charged with power. "I'm twenty-two years old. I'd like to be the one who says what I need and don't need. I'd like to be a part of the conversation." She pointed a finger toward her chest for emphasis. "Instead of all these people deciding for me." She turned and walked back into the hot-tub building.

Elizabeth's mouth dropped open. "I guess I see what you mean."

Gavin shook his head. Once again, Julia's fortitude and courage had surprised him.

Go, Julia.

Julia sat in a chair in the library staring at an ACT practice test resting on a coffee table book that she had propped up with her knee. Ophelia drowsed on her lap. She let out a heavy sigh. She'd done every practice test in the book. Maybe she could borrow Elizabeth's computer and do some online tests. She sighed and pressed her head back against the chair. Doing one more test probably wouldn't make a difference in her score, though. She was so tired of looking at the booklet, she could scream.

Gavin sat across from her, flipping through a book on Yellowstone Park. They had eaten dinner with Elizabeth and then decided to stay in the library until Julia felt tired enough to sleep. She studied him for a moment. The way he narrowed his eyes and licked his lips as he read was endearing.

Julia tapped her foot. She could only study for so

long. Elizabeth said she would fill the hot tub later tonight. Soaking would only consume a small amount of time. Any more of this waiting, and she would go crazy. "So do you think maybe I could go ride the horses or at least go for a walk?"

Gavin looked up from his book. "I know you're restless, but the incident at the hotel told us how serious these people are. I just don't want to take any chances."

She had to trust Gavin's judgment, but sitting around day after day would be impossible to endure.

"So when do I get to finish the trial prep with the Flemings?"

Gavin closed his book and set it on a shelf. He studied her for a moment. "You feel ready for that?"

Julia put the book and practice test on a side table. She turned her head so he wouldn't see her shudder. The memory of the gun against her temple flashed across her mind. Steeling herself against any encroaching fear, she turned to face him.

"Doing nothing makes me more anxious. There's too much time to think. Doing something connected with the trial helps me believe in the possibility that it will all be behind me someday."

He leaned toward her, resting his elbows on his knees. "We need to find a new secure place for you to meet them. The arrangements could take a while. Also, I've got a cousin who works in the prison where Elijah is being kept who's trying to ferret out some information for me. The guys we took into custody from the hotel aren't talking. We need to figure out how Elijah is giving orders from his jail cell. Only his lawyers are allowed to visit him, so he must be working with someone in the prison."

Julia's stomach tightened at the mention of Elijah's name. "That's no surprise. He's pretty good at getting people to do things for him."

Compassion etched across his features. "Talking about him still bothers you, doesn't it?"

Even as she struggled with her fears, the words he had said earlier to Elizabeth floated back into her head. She pushed the cat off and rose from the chair. She faced the bookshelf, afraid of what she might see in his eyes when he answered her question. "Did you mean what you said?"

"Said what?"

She'd heard most of the conversation between them and had been turning it over in her mind ever since. She pulled a book from the shelf and flipped through it, attempting to sound casual. The cat twirled around her feet. "When you were talking to Elizabeth, you said that you thought I was a strong woman."

"I think people underestimate you, Julia. They think because of everything that happened to you, you should be messed up. But I think it has made you stronger and given you an incredible survival instinct. You handled yourself like a champion back at that hotel. You thought strategically when most people would have fallen to pieces. Dropping those beads saved your life."

No one else thought that about her. Up until the day she had left with Gavin, her father had hovered around her. Then again, no one else had seen her in a crisis like Gavin had. "Thank you for believing that about me." She wanted to believe that about herself. Gavin's confidence in her bolstered her hope. When she turned to face him, he had risen from his chair.

His eyes pierced through her. "It's the truth, Julia."

The intensity of his gaze stirred up the affection she

had for him. It was hard to sort through all these feelings. Maybe the blossoming emotions were just because they had been in such close quarters. He had saved her life more than once. Was she mistaking gratitude for attraction?

Elizabeth's words about her attachment to Gavin being unhealthy troubled her. He had probably had clients develop crushes on him before. Were her feelings real or just borne of the threat of danger she had to live with?

She hugged the book she'd picked out to her chest. "I suppose I'll go upstairs and read in my room before I go to bed." Without thinking, she reached out and touched his arm with her free hand.

He stepped back and ran his hands through his blond-brown hair. "That sounds like a good idea."

Something in his tone of voice was guarded. She sensed that he was detaching. She made her way back to the lodge. Gavin's footsteps crunched in the snow behind her. She didn't have to turn around to know he was constantly surveying the surrounding area. His vigilance was a comfort to her.

As they walked beneath a dark sky twinkling with stars, she couldn't help but wish they had met under different—and less traumatic—circumstances.

A sound awoke Gavin from his chair where he drowsed. He sat up straight, and his hand went to his gun. He surveyed the floor below him. It had been the faintest inkling of a noise out of place.

He eased back into the chair, but forced himself to stay awake. Both Elizabeth and Julia had gone to bed hours ago. The wind rattled the windows. A snowstorm was brewing outside, but that hadn't been what he had heard.

His gaze fixated on the doorknob. Had someone been trying to get in?

Then a muffled thump came from the kitchen. He jerked forward in his chair as he unclicked the leather strap that held his gun in the side holster.

He rose to his feet and stood at the edge of the balcony.

Julia's door scraped across the floor. She peeked out. "Is something going on?"

"You're supposed to be sleeping," he said.

"I was, but I heard you moving around out here."

He didn't like that she was sleeping so lightly. Did she not feel safe? "I thought I heard a noise. Probably nothing." He felt that strange prickling at the back of his neck that told him it was something, but he didn't want to feed into her anxiety. "Go back to sleep."

"You're going to go down there and check it out, aren't you?"

Was he that predictable? "As a matter of precaution, I have to investigate. Stay here."

She lifted her chin in defiance, but relented. "Should I lock the door?"

"Yes, and don't open it until I come back—until you hear my voice." He didn't want to alarm her, but Elijah's people liked to operate in pairs. While he was being distracted by one in the kitchen another might find a way to get up to Julia's room. Julia's question indicated that she understood that.

Her eyes pleaded with him. "Hurry back."

"I will." Maybe Elizabeth was right. Her attachment was unhealthy. She needed to trust him. She needed to work with him. But she needed to be able to walk away from him and stand on her own once the trial was over. "Remember what I said about staying away from the window."

She nodded and then slipped back into her bedroom. He heard the deadbolt slide as he pulled his weapon and went down the stairs.

Gun raised, he pushed through the swinging door of the dining hall. He sighted in on each of the four corners of the hall and then, stepping lightly, made his way toward the kitchen. He pushed open the door. It was dark. As he reached for the light switch, he listened but couldn't detect any out-of-place sound. Light illuminated the room. He scanned from one end to the other.

Then he heard scratching from the pantry. When he opened the door, Ophelia meowed at him and strutted out. Gavin shook his head and chuckled. The old *it was the cat* ploy.

Gavin gathered the cat into his arms and walked into the lobby, making sure the doors were closed behind him. "Why don't you stay where I can keep an eye on you?" He placed the animal on her favorite cushion. He made his way back up the stairs and knocked on Julia's door. "Everything is okay. Ophelia was prowling around."

The deadbolt slid back, and Julia opened the door. "Thanks. Good night."

Gavin settled back down in his chair. Still feeling unsettled, he stared at the doorknob for a moment. Had he seen it turn, or had his imagination been fed by a prowling cat?

TWELVE

Julia slipped under the covers and sat up in bed with her book. All the excitement had made her even less sleepy. A few minutes later, she noticed the sound of Elizabeth moving around in the room next to hers. The older woman hadn't poked her head out when Gavin heard the cat noises, but maybe she had been awakened, too.

Julia read until she was drowsy. She reached to turn off the light next to her bed. Outside her door, the familiar and comforting sound of Gavin scooting his chair across the floor helped her fall asleep. She drifted into a deeper rest.

She awoke with a start, fully alert, mind clear. The sheets rustled as she moved from lying on her side to her back. Something felt different. She couldn't hear Gavin's faint snore as he drowsed.

A sliver of light snuck into the room at the base of the door, but she couldn't see if his chair was still there. She lay in bed staring at the ceiling.

Whether it was the noise from a dream or an actual noise, something had caused her to wake up. After lying in bed for a few minutes, it was obvious she wasn't going to be able to go back to sleep right away.

She pulled the covers back, walked into her private bath and splashed cold water on her face. The clock read 2:00 a.m.

She moved back toward her bed, glancing out the window as she stepped past. A flash of movement caught her eye. She stepped toward the window, keeping in mind what Gavin had said about not standing where she was an easy target. She stood off to one side and angled her head so she could look again.

The tall cottonwoods stood like dark sentinels, their bare branches waving in the wind. She scanned the ground below. Moonlight had revealed movement by the trees.

Only allowing half of her face to be visible, Julia stared more intently. She felt a hammer blow to her heart. A figure separated from the trees. The color yellow became more distinctive as the person moved across the yard, then stopped abruptly and lifted her head toward Julia's window.

Julia moved away from the window and pressed her back against the wall. Her heart pounded out a raging beat. A young blond girl who could have been her twin from nine years ago looked up at her.

She felt lightheaded as panic spread through her body. She scrambled toward the door in the dark and fumbled with the knob.

Gavin jumped to his feet and whirled around when the door opened. "What is it?" He grabbed her arm above the elbow.

"I…I…out the window. I saw…a girl…who looked like me." Her bones and joints felt like they were being shaken from the inside.

Gavin's forehead wrinkled. "Are you sure?"

Julia took a step back. He didn't believe her. She

rested a hand against the wall and shook her head. "I wasn't…dreaming it. I know what I saw." Then she realized how absurd what she said sounded. Even as she spoke, doubt entered her mind. Maybe the stress was making it hard for her to separate imagination from reality.

"I'll check it out." He ran the few steps to Elizabeth's door and pounded on it.

"Elizabeth, I need you to stay with Julia."

No answer. He pushed open her door. Elizabeth sat at a desk with her headphones on.

She took the headphones off as concern registered on her face. "What is it?"

"I need to go check something out. Please stay with Julia." Gavin bolted down the stairs.

Julia gripped the railing. What if she was sending Gavin on a wild goose chase?

"Okay, I can do that." Elizabeth's face had gone pale, and her wavering voice revealed the level of fear she was feeling. She gripped her flannel nightgown at the collar. "You think someone might be out there?"

Gavin glanced up at Julia, giving away nothing in his expression. "Julia may have seen something by the cottonwood trees."

Uncertainty assaulted her at every turn. Saying that she had seen a woman in the yard that looked like a younger version of her sounded crazy. The cult members wouldn't send a teenage girl to kill her. "I'm not sure. Maybe it was nothing."

Gavin squared his shoulders. "I need to check out everything." He looked up at Elizabeth. "Lock the door behind me. I have a key."

After Gavin left, Elizabeth swept downstairs and locked the door.

"Let's go to your room," Julia said. She was still disturbed by the image of the young woman she had seen by the cottonwoods. She had no desire to go back to her own room.

Elizabeth came back up the stairs and gathered Julia into her arms. The older woman opened her door, allowing Julia to step into the room first. She turned the lock into place. The light above the desk was on, and the quilt on the bed didn't look as if it had been pulled back.

Julia walked over to the desk, that had an open laptop on it, as well as a pile of papers. "You haven't slept yet?"

"I needed to get some work done. Once the repairs are complete, I'll have to start working on getting my clientele back." Elizabeth settled into a rocking chair. "Just thought I would catch up on some correspondence."

Without pulling the curtain back, Julia snuck a glance out the window. Gavin walked by with his gun drawn. It bothered her that he hadn't believed her about the girl. He had been the one saying all along that she was not emotionally fragile. Was he just telling her that he thought she was strong and capable to give her confidence for the trial, or did he really believe that?

The rocking chair creaked as Elizabeth slipped into it.

Aware that she could be seen from the window if she sat on the bed, Julia slipped down on the floor, using the bed as a backrest. As always, Gavin was diligent about checking out every false alarm, whether it was a cat or a figment of her imagination.

She crossed her arms over her body. The girl had looked so real. If she had just imagined her, it put her back at square one, after two years of counseling. Her mind was still playing tricks on her. "It was probably nothing." Her voice was barely above a whisper.

The minutes ticked by, marked by the creaking of the rocking chair.

Julia checked out the window again by walking on her knees and peering from the bottom. This time she couldn't see Gavin, only the tall cottonwoods and the darkness beyond.

"I hope he's okay out there," Julia said.

Elizabeth wandered over to her laptop, picked it up and sat back down in the rocking chair. "He seems to know what he's doing."

The creaking of the rocking chair and the tapping of the keys on the laptop filled the silence. The longer Gavin was gone, the more she worried. What if somebody was out there? Though Julia's mind raced, she tried to push away any thoughts of bad things happening to Gavin. How long would she wait before she went out there to find him? Even as the tension and fear seeped through her, she knew that she would be more than willing to risk her own life to find him. He had done the same for her over and over.

Elizabeth angled the laptop for a better view of whatever she was reading. "Gavin is a very capable bodyguard, but the more I see of what this job involves, the more I think that this is almost a two-bodyguard job."

"My father could only afford one bodyguard." Most of her father's savings had been wiped out for her counseling. He had sacrificed so much, been through so much. The memory of seeing her father for the first time after seven years returned. At the police station where she had waited after her escape, she had turned to see him as he came through the doors. Her heart had lurched at the sight of her daddy. She rushed over to him, burying herself against his soft, wool shirt as strong arms folded around her.

Even now, the words he said rang through her head. "I never stopped hoping...never stopped praying."

She had felt her father's prayers in the dark moments of her captivity.

Elizabeth's voice broke through her thoughts. "Gavin was willing to step up to the plate and take the job."

"Yeah." Now she wondered why he had taken the job. Her father couldn't be paying him enough to justify all that he had to go through. Elizabeth had gotten way more than she bargained for. Her father had been through so much. Everyone had made sacrifices.

Her resolve to see justice returned. If there had been a setback and the nightmares were back, she would get past them. And she would make it to the trial. If not for herself, then for everyone who had given up so much.

Elizabeth stopped rocking. "I think I'm finally starting to feel tired." She lifted her arms and yawned. "As soon as Gavin gets back, I'm hitting the hay."

As soon as Gavin gets back.

The words ricocheted through her head. "Maybe I should go look for him." She spoke in a whisper.

"No, stay here where it's safe." Elizabeth rose from her chair and pulled a Bible out of a drawer. She got down on her knees so she was facing Julia. "Here, read. Maybe that will help take the worried look off your face."

Julia opened the Bible and read while Elizabeth closed her eyes and rocked in the chair. Julia suspected that the older woman was praying.

She read through several psalms. When she looked up at the antique clock on the wall at least half an hour

Julia entered her room and got into bed without turning on the light or looking out the window. She closed her eyes.

Just as she drifted off to sleep, she heard her name whispered. Julia's eyes popped open. Now she was hearing things. Her eyes welled up with tears. She really was still not ready to face Elijah.

Then she heard it again, a soft whisper. "Julia."

It was real. It had to be. Too afraid to scream, she lay paralyzed in the bed.

She found the strength to sit up. A hand went over her mouth.

THIRTEEN

Gavin positioned his chair in the usual spot. The adrenaline rush from the search had energized him. He'd be able to stay awake for most of the night.

He hadn't meant to doubt what Julia told him, but her assertion that she had seen someone who looked like her in the yard seemed almost like something she'd made up. She'd held it together through the attack at the hotel. Was this a delayed reaction to all of it? Or maybe her father had been right. She was still fragile.

What if he had only wanted to see her as healed and ready for a relationship because he was falling for her? He had to let go of the intense affection he felt for her. The thought of this job being over soon and him not having an excuse to see Julia, to be close to her, made his heart ache.

Her father had said there had been nightmares and that Julia had a hard time being alone because she heard things that weren't there. William Randel hadn't said anything about Julia seeing things, though. It wasn't his job to play psychologist, but it bothered him that he might not have protected her from more emotional trauma. He knew that in desiring to protect her heart and her mind, he'd gone way beyond his job description.

If he couldn't hope for a relationship with her, he could at least take care of her until the trial.

He sat down in the chair and crossed his arms. Two or three years from now, when the trial was a distant memory for Julia, she would cross the path of some lucky guy. He only hoped that guy saw how special she was.

"Don't be alarmed. Please don't scream." The voice was very close to Julia's ear. "I'm going to turn on the light." The hand came off her mouth.

In an instant, Julia found the strength to cry out for Gavin.

The light went on. A blond girl, not more than sixteen years old, stood in front of her. Gavin burst through the door, his weapon drawn. He backed off the second he saw the girl.

The girl stumbled back against a chair, her eyes wild with fear. She drew her hands up protectively in front of her. "Please...please, don't shoot me."

Julia took in a ragged breath. Her heart thudded from all the excitement. She knew this girl from the compound. "Don't be afraid, Lydia. I remember seeing you working in the garden that day Marlena snuck me outside when Elijah was gone. I talked to you." The memory of that spring assaulted her. She had felt the sun on her face and smelled honeysuckle in the air for the first time in months.

Lydia's head jerked as Julia spoke in a calm voice, but she continued to shake and hold her hands up. "Please...please...don't hurt me."

Gavin holstered his weapon and moved toward the girl. "I'm not gonna—"

The girl screamed, the terror in her eyes growing

even more intense. Julia ran over to her and wrapped her arms around her in the same way Marlena had done for her. Lydia was trembling uncontrollably. "It's all right," Julia soothed and then addressed Gavin. "Could you step back outside? You've made her afraid."

"But she could be—"

Julia didn't know why the girl had come, but compassion overwhelmed any suspicion she had. "She's a child. I don't think she's going to hurt me."

Gavin opened his mouth to protest, but then stepped across the threshold, remaining where he could still see Julia.

Elizabeth came to the door. "What on earth is all the noise about?" She rushed over to the two women. "Who is this?"

Lydia wailed. Her head jerked side to side as tears streamed down her face.

"She's from the cult," Julia said.

Gavin loomed in the doorway. "Did you come here by yourself?"

Still panic stricken, Lydia held up her hands, palms out. "I promise you. I came alone."

Elizabeth grabbed Lydia's hands. "What are you doing here?"

"I came to see Julia." The girl shuddered and then swiped at her eyes. "I came for help."

"How did you know where to find me?"

"I heard the men talking about how they knew where you were staying and how they were making plans to come over here."

A sense of urgency Julia had never heard before permeated Gavin's voice. "How did they find out she was here?"

Lydia opened her mouth to speak as shock spread across her face. "I...I don't know."

Gavin continued to stand in the doorway. "That means they know where we are. We have to get out of here." He stepped toward Lydia and locked on to her with his eyes. "What is their plan? When are they coming for Julia?"

Julia straightened her spine. Gavin's direct manner was making Lydia more flustered. Still, she needed to address some of his suspicions. "So why did you come here—to find me?"

"I wanted to warn you and I..." Lydia grabbed Julia's sleeve. "Please, I need your help. They want me to marry Jerry Smith. He must be forty years old."

Lydia's story seemed believable. Elijah rarely picked the younger men for husbands for the teenage girls.

The girl continued. "When I said I didn't want to marry someone that old, my father...my father..." She pulled her shirt away at the shoulder to reveal bruises.

Julia fixated on the purple and black marks. She took a step back as the room spun around her. Gavin was there, holding her, whispering in her ear. "Come on, let's get you out of here."

As Gavin led her out, she heard Elizabeth say, "I can deal with Lydia."

Julia had no memory of how she had gotten down the stairs. Maybe Gavin had carried her. But she found herself sitting on the couch facing the outdoor pool. Gavin brought her a glass of water and sat down beside her.

She had calmed enough to sip the water, but her hands were still shaking. Gavin grabbed one of her hands and pressed it between his palms.

The warmth of his touch seeped into her skin. "I'm okay," she said.

"No, you're not; don't lie to me."

"You're right." Her throat tightened, and she closed her eyes to try to shut out the image of the bruises on Lydia's slender shoulder.

"Did that happen to you?"

"Once, only once. You have to understand what Marlena did for me. How she protected me." Julia shivered as images from the past threatened to consume her. "She took the blows for me. And I left her there."

"You said yourself she was dead when you decided to run." He pressed his palms tighter against her hand. "Your split-second decision probably saved your life."

And there was nothing she could do to bring Marlena back. To give Marlena the chance she had deserved. But she could save Lydia.

Elizabeth came down the stairs and headed toward the kitchen. "She has calmed down a little bit. I'm going to get her some warm milk." She disappeared into the dining hall.

"I have to help Lydia," Julia said.

Gavin lifted his eyes toward the stairs. "We don't have that kind of time. I need to get you out of here." He spoke under his breath. "How do we know she's not part of some plot?"

"She said she came to warn me." She grabbed his shirt sleeve. "They wouldn't send a girl. They want me dead. She had a perfect opportunity to kill me when we were alone in the bedroom and she didn't. If she was part of a plot, they would have given her a weapon."

Gavin stiffened. "I don't know. Don't you think it's weird that a girl who looks a lot like you shows up?"

Gavin could be right. This might be Elijah's way of messing with her head, but she just couldn't see Lydia as the enemy. It didn't make sense that the followers would give them time to escape by first sending Lydia in. "She's barely a teenager and probably not strong enough to overpower me. I understand your suspicions, but we can't turn her out in the cold. We could make some calls, find a safe place for her. She came all this way to me for help."

"Elizabeth is going to have to do that. You and I have to go—tonight. We'll have to move around until we can find a secure location."

As afraid as she was of the cult getting hold of her, Julia hated the thought of leaving Lydia. Though all the cult members watched each other closely, Julia had been the only one under lock and key because Elijah feared she would be spotted by outsiders, and he would be turned in for kidnapping.

Even the adult members had the illusion of being able to come and go as they pleased. The chains that kept them tied to Elijah were inside their heads. Elijah had a way of making the outside world seem so scary that no cult member wanted to leave. Lydia had been raised in the cult. She knew no other life. Her escape showed incredible bravery and determination.

Elizabeth came through the swinging doors of the dining hall just as Lydia appeared at the top of the stairs.

"Would you like to come down, dear?" The older woman held up a glass of milk.

Lydia nodded. She moved cautiously down the stairs as though each step was a fearful choice she had to make.

She sat opposite Julia. Her eyes were red from crying. She folded her hands in her lap and sat up ramrod straight. She was dressed in the approved wardrobe for female cult members. A yellow, calico-print dress that looked as if it was something from the nineteenth century buttoned up to her neck. Her blond hair had been loosened from its tight braids.

Julia still felt as though she was looking in a time-travel mirror, seeing herself as she must have been nine years ago.

Elizabeth set the warm milk on the table in front of Lydia.

"How did you get here, Lydia?" Though suspicion was still evident in Gavin's voice, he asked the question gently.

"I went into town with my mother to sell some wool we had spun into yarn. When she went to the grocery store, I ran away." Lydia wrung her hands as she talked. "I caught rides from Thornburg to Silver Cliff, and then I walked out here." She looked directly at Julia. "Please don't send me back to them."

While Julia understood that the questions had to be asked, Lydia's vulnerability tugged at her heart. "Is there someone we can call for you? Somewhere you can go?"

Lydia smoothed her skirt. "My mom has a sister in California. I haven't seen her since I was little, but maybe she would take me in."

Elizabeth patted Lydia's shoulder. "We'll make some calls in the morning." She pushed the milk closer to her.

"How did you get in?" Gavin's unwavering gaze was making Lydia squirm.

Lydia hung her head as though she had just been scolded. "I pushed the screen out and crawled in through a basement window."

Gavin let out an exasperated sigh. "One of the windows wasn't latched."

"It looked latched, but it was broken. An adult wouldn't be able to fit through." She picked up the milk and took a sip. "I'm small, so it was easy for me to fit. I know I should have knocked. I saw Julia in her room when I was running across the yard. That's how I knew which room to go to. I thought I would find her in there and just talk to her…and then I heard voices and I got scared."

She gave Gavin a wary glance. She was still afraid of him, which wasn't surprising. Lydia probably thought all men were controlling and cruel, like the cult members.

Julia scooted forward on the couch and spoke gently. "Maybe you would be willing to press charges for what happened to you—for the bruises."

Fear entered Lydia's eyes as she pulled back. "Please, I just want to get away. I'm not brave like you."

This wasn't the time to push the frightened girl, but a desire for justice rose up in Julia. She could put Elijah away for murder and kidnapping, but would that be enough? What if the cult continued to exist after that? If only there was some way she could ensure that not one more young woman would have to endure what Lydia had.

Julia rose to her feet. "I understand why you feel that way. You're really scared now. Elizabeth will find a safe place for you to stay."

Lydia grabbed Julia's hand from across the table. "I wish you could help me."

Julia's heart ached as Lydia clutched her hand with delicate, cold fingers. No matter how much she wanted to help this poor girl, she was not in a place where she could. Not tonight, anyway.

"In the morning, I'll get in touch with your aunt."

Elizabeth rose to her feet and faced Gavin. "I guess this means you have to go."

"You should go into town, too." Gavin never took his eyes off Lydia. "Julia, get your things together. I'll meet you at the front door in ten minutes. I'll call your father to see if he can start setting up a new location."

"I wish you didn't have to go." The look on Lydia's face was one of desperation.

"Elizabeth will get you to your aunt." Julia kneeled down so she was facing Lydia. She cupped Lydia's face in her hands. "When this trial is over, I'll do everything I can to help you start a new life."

Julia rose to her feet. A wave of sadness hit her when she looked at the older woman. "I guess we better go."

Elizabeth held her arms open for Julia. "I am so glad I got to know the daughter of my best friend. Next time you come back to the hot springs, it will be for a real vacation."

She was going to miss Elizabeth. As she rested in the embrace, Julia felt as though her world were being ripped apart yet again.

"Lydia." Gavin's voice had an edge to it. "Did you hear the cult members say when they were coming here?"

Lydia stared at the floor. "I think they were waiting to hear from Elijah."

Gavin squeezed Julia's arm just above the elbow. "If that's the case, it might buy us some time." He spoke as though he didn't totally believe Lydia. "All the same, we better hurry."

Julia pulled free of Elizabeth's hug. As she raced up the stairs, she heard Gavin tell Elizabeth he wanted to talk to her. Julia opened her door and stepped into her room. She hardly had anything to pack. She'd lost most of her belongings at the hotel. Panic whirled inside her as she grabbed her toothbrush, a book and a few clothes. She slipped into the winter coat Elizabeth had given her.

When she came down the stairs, Gavin was waiting by the door. Elizabeth came through the sliding glass doors wearing her winter coat and carrying an overnight bag.

Julia stuttered in her step. Lydia was no longer in the room. "What's going on?"

Elizabeth rushed over to Julia. "Lydia is changing into some different clothes that I had on hand."

"Just because we're gone doesn't mean the followers won't show up. I don't want Elizabeth to stay here, and I don't want her to be alone with Lydia," Gavin added. "She's going to drive out ahead of us."

"I will come outside as soon as Lydia is ready," said Elizabeth. The older woman reached up and brushed her fingers over Julia's cheek. "You take care."

Julia offered Elizabeth a faint smile before Gavin ushered her through the door and out to the Mustang. The sky was black, and the air held a chill. Gavin opened his car door but then turned a half circle. His feet crunched on the gravel.

"What is it?" Her voice held a thin, high-pitched quality brought on by fear.

"Get in. Just get in."

Julia slipped into the passenger seat. A moment later, Elizabeth and Lydia came out and got into Elizabeth's car. The taillights glowed red as Elizabeth pulled out of the lot. Gavin started the engine of the Mustang.

He turned the car around and headed toward the road. She craned her neck for one more look at the hot springs as a wave of sadness hit her. Would the day ever come when she wasn't running? She turned back around. Elizabeth's taillights were still visible on the road ahead of them. "You still don't trust Lydia, do you?"

"You're right. It doesn't make sense that they would send someone in to warn us. The whole thing about hitchhiking here seems a little crazy," Gavin said. "I don't know what to think."

Julia lowered her voice. "I understand the kind of determination that would make you hitchhike that far."

"I'm just taking precautions. Elizabeth will see to it that Lydia gets to a safe place. She's going to let the police know that she fears she might have intruders. Maybe they can catch some more of these guys when they show up. Hopefully, we'll be in another county by then, so the media coverage won't hurt us."

Elizabeth's taillights faded out of view.

Already, that sense of being stirred into a frenzy had invaded her awareness. How much longer would they have to be on the run? "Did my father have any ideas about another secure location?"

Gavin let out a heavy sigh. "Our conversation didn't go well. He said he would work with the police on his end to find a place, but I'm afraid the news about us being found has made him afraid…and irrational. He wants you to come home."

"That would be the first place the followers would look."

"Exactly. Your father wants to protect you, but we need a location that is not connected to you in any way." He turned and offered her a smile that warmed her to the core. "We'll get through this."

Julia sat back in the seat. His reassurances calmed her.

Gavin accelerated. The car's headlights illuminated

a short section of road, and then a popping sound surrounded her. She had no time to process what the noise might be.

The car fishtailed. Broken glass sprayed down on her. Metal crunched. She was upside down, and then she lost all sense of where she was in space. Her world went blacker than the night sky.

FOURTEEN

When Julia opened her eyes, darkness enveloped her. It took her a moment to realize that she was hanging upside down by her seatbelt. The followers must have shot at the car, causing a rollover. She'd blacked out. She had no idea how much time had passed. If there had been time for them to come and pull her out, why hadn't they? Maybe she had only been unconscious for a few minutes, and they were still running up the road looking for the wrecked car.

She stretched her hand toward the driver's side. "Gavin?"

Slowly, her eyes adjusted to the darkness. Gavin's door had been pushed open. That didn't make sense. Why would the followers take Gavin and not her?

The seatbelt dug into her torso. She fumbled for the clip and pressed down on it. She fell, putting her hand out just before she hit the crumpled roof of the Mustang. Her gloves protected her from the broken glass.

She felt around for the latch to open her door, but when she pressed down and pushed on it, it didn't budge. The hood looked as though it had been crushed on her side. She'd have to get out through the driver's side door. She twisted around in the confined space as the memory of other small dark spaces bombarded her, threatening to paralyze her. If only Gavin were here.

A long-buried Bible verse surfaced. *I can do all things through Christ who strengthens me.*

She could do this alone if she had to. Broken glass dug into her knees and hands as she crawled toward the open door with the verse echoing in her head. She reached out. Her gloved hand touched the snow.

Once outside, Julia reached through the broken window on the passenger side, feeling around for her bag and cell phone, to no avail.

She stood up and placed her hands on her hips. Despair and panic warred inside her. "Gavin?" She waited in the silence. She had no idea where he was or what had happened to him. Had the cult members hurt him? The darkness surrounding the car didn't allow her to search around the area.

She turned, debating her next move. Elizabeth's tail-lights had faded out of view. If she had seen the accident, she would have come back. That left only two options—eihter she'd driven on into town, or she'd been shot at, too.

The lights from the lodge were still visible. There would be a phone there. Maybe she could crawl through the same window Lydia had, or perhaps Elizabeth had left a door unlocked. Pushing down the fear that something had happened to Gavin and Elizabeth, she ran back toward the lodge.

Aware that the followers might check along the road when they didn't find her in the car, she slipped into the shelter of the trees, keeping her eyes on the lights of the lodge as they bobbed in and out of view. Her feet pounded on the hard earth.

By the time she stepped out of the trees on to the

gravel parking lot, her heart was racing. The outdoor lights were on, as well as the lights inside the lodge, but when she tried the door, it was locked.

Snow swirled around the lights and fell softly against Julia's cheeks. The silence was eerie, foreboding.

She tried the kitchen door without success. This would be the one time Elizabeth actually remembered to lock all the doors. If Elizabeth did make it into town, would she call the cell and be alarmed when Gavin didn't answer? She didn't have much time before the followers widened their search to the lodge.

She couldn't remember if there had been a phone in the hot-tub room or not, but it was worth a try. Her hands wrapped around the doorknob. She took in a breath and prayed.

Please God, let this one be open.

The knob turned and she stepped inside. She wandered the expanse of the room, looking for a phone. Elizabeth had gotten around to filling the hot tub they had cleaned. When she tilted her head, snow landed softly on the sky light.

A faint, indiscernible noise came from the library. Treading as softly as she could, she made her way toward the library and pushed the door open.

Gavin crashed through the forest, scanning the area in front of him for any sign of the cult members. His head throbbed from where he had been hit. How long had it been since he had left Julia in the car? Ten minutes, tops.

After the crash, he had had time to press his fingers against her neck, where her pulse pounded out a steady rhythm. She was alive. It had taken only seconds for the followers to get to the car. They pulled on Julia's door, shaking the car, but they couldn't open it.

He drew his gun as he crawled out the driver's side door, only to be greeted with a kick to the head. Gavin scrambled to his feet to overtake his attacker. Another man jumped him from behind, hitting him with an object. He couldn't tell what. A baseball bat? A crow bar? He didn't know. His gun fell somewhere in the grass.

"Just give us the woman, and we'll let you go."

"You'll have to kill me first." Gavin managed a right cross to one of the man's jaws. He lifted his leg for a roundhouse kick to the other man's stomach. The man dodged the kick, and Gavin's foot landed on the man's hand. The object he had been hit with went flying into the trees. It took Gavin a second to comprehend that the object was a rifle. Probably the same rifle they'd used to cause the car accident.

Injuries from the car accident and the blows to the head weakened him. As one of the men raised a fist to him, Gavin grabbed the man's wrist, spun him in a half circle and flipped him on the ground. When Gavin looked up, the other man was running away into the trees.

The man on the ground scrambled to his feet and ran into the trees as well. Gavin chased them far enough into the forest to know they would not come back before he could pull Julia out.

But the head injuries had disoriented him and cost him precious minutes in getting back to her. When he returned to the car, she was gone. As he rested his hands on the upturned car, his heart sank. Had there been others watching the road besides the two he had run off?

Frantic, Gavin raced around the car, attempting to read the tale of the footprints in the snow. A light snow swirled out of the sky, and he noticed the night chill. He was able to discern where he had struggled in the snow with the two men. He couldn't see anything that indicated her body had been dragged. It was nearly impossible to make out anything else in the dim light. He wasted precious minutes looking for his gun and the rifle. No luck.

The search for his cell phone, which he had left on the console, proved fruitless. What had become of Julia? Had she gotten out on her own and gone up to the road to get help? Or had she returned to the lodge?

Maybe Elizabeth had looked back and seen the car crash—if she hadn't been shot at, too.

He had a decision to make, and every second counted.

Julia treaded lightly toward the library door and slowly pushed it open. Lydia sat in a chair crying, with her face in her hands.

Shock registered in her expression when she looked up and saw Julia. She burst out of the chair. "What are you doing here?"

"I might ask you the same thing. Why did you come back here? Where is Elizabeth?" Already, she had a creeping sense that Lydia hadn't been entirely sincere. Still, the girl had a vulnerable quality that Julia felt herself responding to. She couldn't see Lydia as evil, not like the men who wanted her dead.

Lydia's gaze dropped to the floor as her voice filled with shame. "When Elizabeth stopped the car to pull up on the main road, I jumped out and ran back here."

"Why?"

"I wasn't supposed to go into town. That wasn't part of the plan. They're supposed to come and get me here."

"You didn't hitchhike here, did you?" She had so wanted to believe Lydia's story.

Tears streamed down Lydia's face. "They said if I did this, if I flushed you out—" Lydia said the phrase as though it was unfamiliar to her, something she had picked up from the men who put her up to this "—I wouldn't have to marry Jerry Smith."

"Why didn't they just come and get me at the hot springs?"

"They didn't know where you were being kept. And they wanted to make sure Gavin wasn't part of the equation. That's how they said it to me. They said they just wanted to talk you out of testifying."

Now she saw how Lydia's naiveté had been her undoing. The attack at the hotel showed that the followers weren't interested in a negotiation. They wanted her dead.

Their plan made sense. If the car accident didn't kill both of them right away, it would probably incapacitate both her and Gavin long enough for the cult members to move in. They'd seen firsthand at the hotel that Gavin was tenacious and smart in his protection of her. She shuddered. What if they had succeeded in the first part of their plan? And Gavin lay dead or dying in the forest? It had been too dark to search the area around the car.

Pushing down encroaching anxiety about Gavin, she tried to come up with a plan. "I don't suppose Elizabeth had a chance to call the police."

Lydia shook her head. "She jumped out of the car and shouted for me after I ran into the trees. I don't know what happened to her after that."

They had no car, no way of escaping. Julia had a feeling that it would only be a matter of time before the followers came back here looking for her. They might still be coming back for Lydia, even though their plan had been foiled. "How did you get in here, anyway?"

Lydia held up a key ring. "I grabbed these out of Elizabeth's car before I ran. I came in here because that was the first key I got to work."

Julia reached for the keys. "We need to call the police. There's a landline in the lodge. And then we are going to hide until the police get here, and you are not leaving my sight."

At first Lydia nodded, looking contrite as she handed Julia the keys. But then her expression changed as her gaze shifted and settled on a point beyond Julia's shoulder. Lydia's mouth formed a perfect "o." Her face drained of color and fear entered her eyes.

Julia whirled around in time to see a follower raising a hammer up to hit her head. She angled away, and the hammer grazed her shoulder.

Lydia screamed.

Julia lunged at the man, barreling toward his torso. The man fell to the hard, tile floor, groaning. The hammer skittered into the darkness.

While Julia scrambled to her feet, Lydia continued to scream and protest. Julia raced toward the door. Just as her fingers reached out for the knob, a claw-like hand grabbed her shirt collar and pulled her back. Unable to break free, she was dragged across the floor. She tried to twist away and then to reach out, hitting and scratching. Her efforts made little difference. The accident had made her weak. He banged her head against something hard, which left her disoriented as the room spun around her. Her limbs felt as though they were filled with helium.

She felt herself being lifted up and plunged into water. She drifted down. He was going to drown her. Her survival instinct renewed her will to fight. Every time she struggled to raise her head to the water's surface, he pushed it back down. Water splashed. She kicked her legs, flailed her arms. She was not going to die. Not here, not now.

Finally, she stopped fighting, feigning unconsciousness. The pressure on her head let up. She could only hold her breath for a couple minutes.

Summoning all of her strength, she burst out of the water and scrambled to get out of the side opposite from where the man was standing.

Arms wrapped around her waist. She wrenched away from the man's grasp and fell forward into the water. Her head went under face forward, and she sucked in water. She bobbed to the surface, then felt her head being pushed down again.

Right before the water engulfed her, she heard Lydia say, "You promised not to hurt her."

Oh, Lydia, did you really believe them?

The man's hold on her was loose enough that she angled her body and slipped free of his hands, but not before he grabbed her hair. She rose above the water's surface, gasping for air.

The man wrapped his arm around her neck, so her chin rested in the crook of his elbow, immobilizing her. The blended smell of dirt and pine that all the men of the cult seemed to carry around filled her nostrils. The odor flooded her mind with ugly memories and weakened her resolve. As the man squeezed his forearm against her breathing tubes, the will to fight left her. She saw spots before her eyes. Her arms went limp.

"Who do you think you are that you can take down Elijah True?" He pulled his arm back, straining her neck and making it hard to breathe.

She wheezed in a sliver of air. The man was right. Who was she to stand up to Elijah True? Blackness encroached on the rim of her vision. She was tired, so tired of fighting.

Lydia's voice came from far away. "You promised."

"Shut up and submit to my authority." The man spat out the words.

She felt herself becoming dizzy and lightheaded as Lydia's voice grew stronger. "But you promised."

The man held on but loosened his grip slightly. Julia twisted free. An image of Lydia pulling on the man's arm and screaming a protest flashed across her vision. The man turned, grabbed Lydia's face and squeezed it with his hand. "I told you to listen to me. You stupid girl." He pushed on her face, sending her backward.

Julia watched in horror as Lydia fell to the floor. Half moon marks on her face, some of them bleeding, revealed where the man had dug his fingernails in.

Seeing Lydia sent a new surge of rage through her. She knew who she was. She was the person who was going to stop Elijah from poisoning men's minds into thinking it was okay to treat a young girl that way.

Seizing the opportunity, Julia quickly splashed to the other side of the hot tub. The man's hands scraped her back. He ran around to her side of the tub as she lifted her leg to get out. He pulled on her arm and sent her tumbling to the hard, tile floor. Pain exploded through her whole body.

The man lunged toward her and wrapped his arms

around her neck. Even in the dim light, she could see yellow in his eyes. His bitter breath stained her face as she struggled to get away.

"Get off her," a voice roared somewhere in the darkness. Gavin. He pulled the man by his collar and slammed him against the floor, yanking his hands behind him. "Something to tie him up with," he demanded.

It took a moment for Julia to process what Gavin was saying. She struggled to her feet and looked around. The belt from a spa bathrobe would do. She handed it to Gavin, who tied the man's hands behind him. The man on the floor groaned, but didn't struggle.

Gavin spoke through gritted teeth. "I want answers. How did you find us?"

The man was silent for a moment, but then answered with a weak voice. "A woman at the clinic alerted us. We've been patrolling the area ever since, in a wider and wider circle from the clinic. Then I overheard the clerk at the Silver Cliff grocery store mention that the hot springs lady was buying a lot of groceries for one person."

Gavin rose to his feet and looked at Julia. His eyes communicated compassion. She collapsed into his arms, resting against him, trembling and afraid. He made soothing sounds and stroked her wet hair. Her mind calmed, even though her heart was still racing.

He rubbed her back. "Get some dry clothes. We have to go."

She pressed her face against his chest. Julia relished the safety of his arms, but knew it couldn't last. She pulled away and looked into his eyes. "But we don't have a car. Unless Elizabeth came back. Did you see her?"

Gavin shook his head. "I don't know what happened to Elizabeth. They have at least two other cars patrolling that road that I could see. We can't get out that way."

"How are we going to escape?"

"We'll take the horses and head through the back end of the property. The horses put us at an advantage. If they follow us, they'll be on foot." He picked the keys up off the floor where they had fallen. "I'll call the police from the landline, but we cannot afford to wait around for them." He pointed to the follower tied up on the floor. "There were two guys who tried to pull you out of that car to kill you. I don't know where the other one went."

Julia shuddered. The followers were closing in fast.

He grabbed her hand and pulled her toward the door. "Let's get out of here as fast as we can."

She stopped, her gaze darting around the room. "What happened to Lydia?" Despite Lydia's betrayal, Julia felt only sympathy for her. She lived a life where her only option to protect herself from an abusive, love-less marriage was to turn on Julia.

"She wasn't here when I came in." He leaned toward her. "Julia, we can't wait. We'll tell the police about her."

He glanced down at the subdued man on the floor. "Maybe this one will talk, and we can figure out how Elijah is getting his messages out."

The man stared at the floor, his voice filled with venom. "Do you think one weak woman is going to defeat Elijah?"

His words caused ice to form in her veins. Gavin grabbed her hand and squeezed it. His touch renewed her strength. She steeled herself against the threat. No matter what, she wasn't going to let Elijah into her head again.

They raced into the lodge and Gavin called the police while Julia found dry clothes and searched for a map that would show what was on the other side of Elizabeth's acreage and anything else that might be useful. The map was easy enough to find. She also located a flashlight. .

Gavin hung up the phone. "Good news. Elizabeth made it to the police station. The police are on their way."

While Julia unfolded the map she had found, Gavin phoned his friend Brandon. It sounded as though he was making arrangements for a cell phone and a car.

"There's a little town called Madison just on the other side of Elizabeth's property," Julia offered as she heard Gavin struggling to come up with a meeting place. She handed him the open map and pointed to the town. Gavin finished the conversation and hung up the phone. He studied the map for a moment. "You do know how to ride?"

Julia nodded. "I had a horse named Sparkles from the time I was six until the kidnapping."

He grabbed her hand and raced toward the barn through the snow. The scent of hay and manure greeted them as they stepped inside. Julia shone the flashlight she had found. Five horses stood in stalls. A black horse with a white stripe down its nose caught her eye. "I'll take this one."

Gavin located the tack. They worked silently, putting on the bridles and saddle blankets. Their breath was visible in the cold barn. Gavin helped her toss the heavy saddle on her horse's back. She had just cinched up the saddle strap when a venom-filled voice behind her caused her to freeze in her tracks.

"Well, hello there, Julia."

Oct. 3 /21/

FIFTEEN

Gavin whirled around. On instinct, he reached for his gun, then remembered that he'd lost it in the fight after the car crash. Even in the dim light, Gavin recognized the man standing in the doorway as one of the cult members who had tried to pull Julia out of the car.

The man grinned and held up a knife that looked as if it had come from Elizabeth's kitchen.

He heard Julia gasp behind him.

"Get on your horse."

"I wouldn't do that if I were you." The man with the knife stalked toward her. Gavin intercepted him, grabbed the man's wrist and squeezed the pressure points that caused the knife to fall to the ground. As Gavin struggled with the man, he saw Julia in his peripheral vision, trying to mount the horse as it walked sideways and jerked its head up and down to show agitation.

Gavin dropped the man to the dirt floor of the barn so he landed on his stomach. He moved a few paces to grab some baling wire. The man tried to get to his feet, but not before Gavin placed a foot on his back. "The police will be here soon enough for you." He tied the man's hand and feet.

"Not before the others get here!" the man shouted.

Yet another reason why they couldn't wait for the police. The man's threat chilled Gavin to the bone. Julia had already led her horse out of the barn and was trotting toward the open gate of the corral. Gavin got on his own horse and caught up with her.

Once they were free of the corral, they spurred the horses into a gallop. They came to a moonlit meadow that Gavin recognized from the map. Julia leaned forward in the saddle and got up more speed with her horse. They rode hard for at least an hour until the trail narrowed and the forest grew thicker.

Gavin pulled up on the reins. "We can't go fast through this. Even if the followers get there before the police do, they won't be able to catch up with us on foot." Gavin's mind whirled with thoughts of what he had to do in the next six to eight hours. Once they got to Madison and got another car from Brandon, where was he going to take Julia? Where would she be safe?

The horses plodded forward through the darkness as Gavin contemplated their next move. Julia's horse had taken the lead. From the way her head tilted sideways, Gavin could tell she was sleeping. She had been through so much. And yet, she held up and remained strong.

He couldn't do anything until he had a cell phone. Faced with the failure of not being able to get Julia to safety reminded him again of his friend, Joshua. He wondered what Joshua was doing with his life now that he couldn't race. He regretted leaving Florida so quickly, but still wasn't sure he would ever be ready to face his friend. Just thinking about it caused guilt to wash through him.

Julia slipped in her saddle but caught herself. His

horse moved forward at a trot, so he could come up beside Julia. "Are you getting tired?"

"Yes, I've just got to remember not to fall into too deep a sleep." She straightened in the saddle, but he could hear the weariness in her voice. Julia was exhausted.

"Why don't you ride with me? I can lead your horse."

"I don't want to slow us down," she said.

"We'll be fine as long as we just keep moving." He brought his horse to a halt, then reached out and grabbed her reins. "I'd feel better knowing you were rested."

"You mean for whatever we might have to deal with up ahead." Her breath was visible in the dark, cold air.

"Yes." Gavin scooted forward in the saddle. He had to be honest with her. Once they made an appearance in public, there was risk involved.

"You're probably right." She slipped off her horse and placed her foot in Gavin's stirrup while he grabbed her inside arm above the elbow. She settled behind him, wrapping her arms around his waist.

"Comfortable?"

"Yes." She pressed her cheek against his shoulder blade. "Hope I can sleep."

He patted her hand. Within moments, the weight against his back had increased, and he knew she was resting. The horses' hooves clopped through the snow. Only the occasional jingling of the metal in their bridles as they tossed their heads broke the silence.

Gavin tried to pray. Praying for Julia's safety, that he would find a place to take her, was easy. The possibility of not being able to get Julia to safety made him think of past failures. An image of Joshua lying unconscious in the hospital bed invaded his thoughts. His bad decisions as a bodyguard had led to his friend being in that hospital. When the doctor's prognosis was that Joshua would walk with a limp, but would never have the reflexes he needed to race again, Gavin was overwhelmed by guilt. Joshua was better off without him. He'd booked his flight back to Montana the next day.

His faith had come alive that night in the hospital chapel. Gavin had never doubted that faith, but over and over he prayed for God to take the guilt about Joshua away, and He never did. That part of God was hard to understand.

Julia stirred and made a soft moaning sound. The weight on his back lifted.

"How close are we?" she whispered.

"Horses aren't moving real fast. I would guess another two or three hours before we come to the road that leads into Madison." Gavin clicked the light on his watch. 2:00 a.m. His friend had said he could get there by five. If they timed it right, Brandon wouldn't be waiting for long.

Madison didn't look like a very big place on the map. A stranger in town would be easy enough to remember. Two people showing up on horseback would be close to unforgettable. They would be getting there before most people were awake, so that worked in their favor. Besides, as good as the followers had been at tracking Julia, they couldn't be everywhere.

Even though he still needed to come up with a place for them to go, he was confident that this plan would work. It had to.

Julia woke from her sleep. She sat up a little straighter behind Gavin. The warmth she'd felt as she rested against his back faded. "I suppose I should get on my own horse, and we can pick up the pace."

"If you feel alert enough to do that." He tilted his head. "Looks like the trees thin out a little bit up ahead, so we might be able to get up some speed."

He stopped his horse and Julia slipped off. He handed her the reins for her horse, which stepped to one side when she got on. "So do you have any ideas of where we can go?"

He shook his head. "We might just have to drive for a while."

"How will we finish the trial prep?" They were running out of time. What if Elijah won in the end, not because he had kept her out of the courtroom, but because the constant threat had forced the prosecutors to put together a less than perfect case?

"I don't know," he said.

Though his voice had slipped into a monotone, she picked up on the anxiety underneath. They were both worried.

They rode on through the gray light of early morning, pushing the horses into a gallop once they got to a dirt road. The town of Madison appeared as they emerged from behind a stand of trees.

A post office, a bar and a bank came into view. They passed a few houses, all of which had darkened windows.

"My friend said he would meet us by the grain elevators. They're the most visible landmark. He's seen them from the road when he's driven by. We kind of stick out like a sore thumb here. It would be best if we veer off this main street as quickly as possible."

He made a clicking sound, shifted the reins on the horse's neck and turned. Julia followed. The horses' hooves clopped on the concrete. A man leaning against the back bumper of a Jeep stood up as they approached.

A second truck with a horse trailer attached and a woman sitting inside was parked close to the Jeep. Gavin dismounted and drew his friend into a bear hug. "Thanks for helping out." He turned to face Julia, beaming. "Julia, this is Brandon Page."

Brandon shook Julia's hand enthusiastically. "I don't see this guy for ten years and now he just can't get enough of me." He addressed Gavin. "I'm running out of cars to loan you, buddy."

"Looks like you are fresh out of classics. Bring me this old piece of junk now," Gavin cajoled as he kicked the tires on the Jeep.

"It'll get you where you need to go, my friend." Brandon had a smile that took up most of his face.

"Spoken like a true salesman," Gavin said.

Though the two men were joking, Julia could feel the thread of tension that wove through every word. Despite the calm of early morning, they were on the run.

Gavin's expression turned serious. "Sorry about the Mustang. I will make it up to you."

Brandon shrugged. "We'll figure it out later. You've got enough on your mind." Brandon pulled a set of keys and a cell phone out of his pocket and handed them to Gavin. He pointed toward the truck. "So my wife and I will load the horses and take them back to the hot springs."

"That's the plan." He turned back toward Julia. "I need to call your father and let him know the new cell number. Maybe he's found us a place we can go." Gavin stepped away from Julia and Brandon.

After a moment of silence, Julia approached Brandon. "You knew Gavin in high school?"

Brandon nodded and grinned. "Yeah, he was a wild one."

"Really?" She turned to study Gavin. His posture stiffened as he spoke on the phone. The conversation with her father sounded heated. "He's so responsible now. I'm having a hard time picturing him as a reckless teenager."

"Don't get me wrong. He was disciplined. The only teenage black belt I ever met. But he did like to drive cars fast. Got a lot of speeding tickets."

"Oh, yeah?" Gavin had shared very little about his life. She had to admit she was curious to know more.

"Oh, yeah, he and Joshua Van Dyken were the wild boys of Fremont High and as close as brothers." Brandon patted his chest. "I, of course, was a member of the chess club and Future Farmers of America."

"Who was Joshua?"

"Just a friend from high school." Gavin joined them. "Are you telling lies about me again, Page?" He fake punched his friend in the shoulder.

"How did the talk with my father go?" Julia asked.

Gavin's jaw hardened. "Fine."

Judging from his tone, it had gone far from fine.

Brandon broke the tension. "All right, my friend." He held out a hand for Gavin to shake and then slapped him on the back. He winked at Julia. "Take good care of this pretty lady."

Julia blushed and wondered what Gavin had said about her to Brandon.

The two of them got into the car. Gavin took out the map they had found at the hot springs and studied it. A light came into his eyes. "I think I know where we can go."

"Where?" Julia relaxed a little.

"An island on Crystal Lake. I know someone who lives there. I'll have to call him." Gavin started the engine and turned the vehicle around. "But first let's get away from here. This is the only town bordering Elizabeth's property. It will be the first place the cult members look."

When Julia checked her side-view mirror, she saw Brandon standing beside her horse, running a hand over his neck. His dark-haired wife got out of the truck and led Gavin's horse toward the trailer.

They drove along the darkened highway. "Did you say something to Brandon about me?"

"Why?"

"I was wondering what that wink meant when we left."

Gavin kept his eyes on the road in front of him. "When I went to get the Mustang from him, I might have mentioned that I thought you were...pretty."

Julia nodded. So he was talking about her to his friends. She wasn't sure what to do with that information. Again, she found herself wishing that they had met at church or in a college classroom, not under such stress-filled circumstances.

"So you were kind of a wild boy in high school," Julia teased.

Color rose in Gavin cheeks, and he flipped his sunglasses up on his head and then back down. It was the first time she had ever seen Gavin embarrassed. "That was a long time ago," he said dismissively.

"You know so much about me because my story was all over the newspaper. I've shared things with you, but I know hardly anything about you."

"Not much to tell. Born and raised in Montana. Two brothers, one sister. Mom taught fourth grade." Gavin put his sunglasses back on top of his head. Her probing was still making him nervous.

"And in high school you hung out with Brandon… and a guy named Joshua."

A shadow seemed to fall across his face. "The guy whose island we're going to is Joshua's dad. His name is Larry." He leaned forward and then back, wiggling against the back of the driver's seat. "I didn't even think about food. Are you hungry?"

Gavin was pretty adept at changing the subject. He really didn't want to share much about his personal life with her. Over and over, he made it clear that he wanted to keep things professional. Yet she couldn't let go of the idea that he was hiding his feelings, and now he was talking about her to his friends. "How far is it?" She struggled to keep her voice neutral. Trying to figure out Gavin Shane was exasperating.

"We've got a good three- or four-hour drive. If at all possible, I'd like to just drive straight through. I'll have to stop to make the call to Larry. We can get food then if we need to. If you will recall, every time we stop something seems to go wrong, so we should keep that to a minimum."

"I'm with you. The less times we have to stop, the better." She crossed her arms and pressed her back against the seat.

"I can put the radio on if you like," he offered.

"That's okay. We probably can't get a decent radio station out here, anyway."

"You warm enough? I can turn up the heat."

Her mind reeled back to when he had asked the same questions the first day they were together in the car. So much had changed since then—for her, anyway. "No, I'm not cold. Thanks."

He tapped his thumbs on the steering wheel. "Anything you want, just let me know."

I want to know if you have the same feelings for me as I have for you. That's what I want, Gavin.

Julia laced her fingers together and turned her head toward the window so Gavin wouldn't see the tears in her eyes.

SIXTEEN

Gavin hit the turn signal and veered off on a side road. Crystal Lake came into view. Snow-capped mountains jutted up around the huge lake. Early morning light made it glisten like silver.

When he had made the call, Larry Van Dyken had heartily agreed to take them in. Despite Larry's enthusiasm, Gavin had still felt trepidation about seeing the father of the man whose career he had destroyed. He had to let go of his own fears. This was not about him. The island was the safest place for Julia—it was remote, and no one would connect it to her. If he hadn't seen Crystal Lake on the corner of the map, it would not have occurred to him that the island was an option.

He slowed the car and peered through the trees. "There's a turnoff for a dock somewhere here."

The Jeep rolled down a dirt road to a dock.

Julia peered over the dashboard. "There's no boat."

"Larry doesn't leave the boat out here where anyone could take it. He said he'd meet us and take us to the island." Gavin checked his watch. "I gave him a window of time for when we could get here. He should show up any minute."

At least the call to Larry had gone smoother than the

one he had to make to Julia's father. His conversation with William Randel had been short and to the point when her father had again insisted that he bring Julia back home.

He outlined all that had happened since their last call, but brushed over the attack on Julia in the hot-tub room. "Mr. Randel, Julia and I are on the move. Your daughter's life is in extreme peril. I know that you are concerned about her, but bringing her back there is not an option. The closer we get to this trial…"

"Where are you taking her?" Even across the phone William's distress was evident.

"I don't know yet." If only he had thought of Larry Van Dyken's island before he'd called William. Maybe that would have eased the older man's anxiety.

A long pause on the other end of the line indicated William was trying to work through something. "What you say makes sense. I know she can't come back here. It's just that I wish I could see her, see that she is okay." William Randel's voice cracked. "How is she? How is Julia holding up?"

"Your daughter is a remarkable woman." He struggled to keep the emotion out of his voice as a realization spread through him. He loved Julia.

William said, "I hate being away from her."

Gavin debated telling William Randel that his daughter was not the weak creature he viewed her as. The idea of asking her father if he could go back on the promise he had given warred within him. More than anything, he wanted Julia to know how he felt about her.

He thought better of it. What if William's reaction was to fire him? He couldn't risk not being close to her. He wouldn't trust another man to protect her. "Julia has held up really well. Anybody else would have fallen apart. We're going to get her to that trial and see to it that the rest of her life is very ordinary."

William took in an audible breath as though he were garnering strength to say what needed to be said. "If that's the way it has to be. I am putting my daughter's life in your hands. I know you probably can't communicate while you are en route, but please let me know when you are at your safe location. I need to at least hear her voice."

"I will, and I'm sure Julia will want to talk to you then, too." Gavin hung up.

Now as they waited at the dock for Larry's boat to show up, he knew he had made the right choice. If he was to have a relationship with Julia, he wanted William Randel's blessing. Maybe after the trial, he could talk to him.

Julia stared out at the lake. There were still patches of snow along the bank. "I remember coming here when I was a little girl."

Gavin pulled the keys out of the ignition. "Really?"

"My mom and dad and I camped overnight. It was summertime. We built a campfire. My dad played his guitar."

"That's a good memory."

Julia leaned back in the seat. "I can hear Daddy's voice and see the flicker of firelight across my mother's face." She let out a breath and shook her head. "I never would have remembered that if we hadn't come back here." She closed her eyes. "I'm glad we came here already."

"Happy to oblige." He'd dragged her halfway across the countryside and she still found something positive, despite the muddled mess her life was.

"It's easy for the bad memories to overwhelm the

good." Still resting her head against the back of the seat, she turned to look at him. Her blue eyes drew him in.

His heart quickened when he looked at her. "But you managed to find a good memory."

"I've had practice. When Elijah would lock me in a closet for punishment, and I had to sit there in the dark, I'd ask God to bring a good memory into my head."

"What kind of memories did you come up with?"

"Little things, like how different kinds of ice cream tasted. Christmas Eve service at church."

She continued to look at him, and he could not free himself of the magnetic pull of her gaze. He dropped his eyes to her mouth. The desire to kiss her was almost too much. His mouth had gone dry. "Julia."

"Yes."

He straightened in his seat, pulling himself free of the electrical charge of the moment. "I'm impressed with who you've become, despite all you have been through." He couldn't bring himself to look at her. It took all his willpower to push down the attraction he felt.

He peered through the windshield and tapped his fingers on the steering wheel. A boat came around a corner. "Looks like our ride is here." He pushed open the door and stepped outside, grateful to put some distance between him and Julia. His willpower was wearing down.

Larry Van Dyken's red winter cap, with the mass of snowy, white hair sneaking out from underneath, was the first thing to come into focus. Tension wound through Gavin's torso. He wouldn't be facing Joshua, but something about having to look his father in the eye made him apprehensive.

Let it go. This has to be about Julia.

The boat slowed as it drew nearer.

"Is that the guy?" Julia stood beside Gavin.

"Oh, yeah, I think Larry's had that Einstein hair since Joshua and I were in high school."

Larry stepped out on the dock and tied off the boat. He straightened his back and buttoned the down vest he wore before ambling toward them. He offered them an infectious grin.

He held out a hand for Gavin to shake. "Gavin Shane. You crazy kid."

Gavin shook the older man's hand, but stiffened when he was pulled into a hug. Gavin took a step back. "This is Julia."

Julia adjusted the bag she had managed to throw together before they fled. "Pleased to meet you." She held out a hand.

"I've got blankets in the boat. When we get going and that cold wind hits you, you'll want to cover up."

They settled into the boat. The tall waders Larry wore allowed him to step into the water to push off while Gavin started the motor. Larry jumped into the boat as it took off.

"Do you remember the way, son?"

Gavin turned to face the father of the man whose life he had destroyed. Guilt and shame rose to the surface. He didn't deserve to be called *son*. "I can manage," he said flatly.

Julia pulled a wool, plaid blanket up to her neck as the boat picked up speed. Gavin's eyes watered from the cold air hitting him. The chill invigorated him, and he navigated the boat around a peninsula populated with bare deciduous trees and patches of snow.

Larry gave directions as they headed out into open water and traveled with only one side of the shoreline visible. The sparkling lake stretched on forever. The energy it took to brace against the chill loosened some of the tension knotted inside him.

The house came into view. The island was about three acres across with a single dock. The house, constructed of red brick, had a colonial look to it with its columns and big front porch. Gavin brought the boat into the dock.

Larry jumped out. "Got some wooden planks for you to walk on so you don't have to get your feet wet."

Gavin got out, sinking one boot into the water in the process to help Larry lay down the boards so Julia could step out.

The older man led the way up a series of stone steps to the house. "Gavin asked that I send the hired help away. I've been a widower for three years, so it's just me here." The older man had a twinkle in his eyes as he addressed Julia.

They stepped inside the house. A fire crackled in the fireplace of the great room, and a tea service had been set on the coffee table. The scent of cinnamon wafted down the hallway from the kitchen. Gavin stepped in behind Julia.

"This is really nice," Julia said.

"Have a seat," Larry encouraged.

The room was much as Gavin had remembered it from the last time he had visited. Larry was the kind of man who thrived on the world staying the same. Julia settled into an overstuffed chair by the fireplace.

"If you'll excuse me for a moment, I can warm up those sweet rolls." Larry disappeared down a long hallway.

Gavin moved toward the warmth of the fire, but stopped short when he saw the photographs on the mantel. The first was of Joshua in his racing uniform. The second was of Joshua with an arm around his wife, standing next to his race car.

Gavin felt as though he had been punched in the stomach.

"You'll have to excuse me. I need some air." He rushed outside.

As the door closed behind Gavin, Julia sat stunned. Though she had seen an obvious change in emotion in his expression, he had left so quickly she had no idea what had triggered the change.

She sat back in the chair. He never left her side so arbitrarily. Maybe he just felt more relaxed now that they were safe on the island. Still, it was out of character for him.

Larry appeared in the doorway holding a plate of rolls. He took a seat opposite her. "Enjoy."

"Those look yummy."

"Where did Gavin go?"

"He went outside. I'm not sure why." Julia grabbed one of the rolls and stood up to look at the photos on the fireplace mantel. She leaned toward a photo of a young woman embracing a child in each arm.

"That is my daughter, Alison, and my two grandkids, Joe and Maggie. They come out here in the summer to wear me out."

She picked up the photo of a man in a racing uniform.

Larry moved closer to Julia. "That's my son, Josh."

"Oh, yeah, he was Gavin's friend from high school."

"He was more than that. Gavin was his bodyguard for over two years."

"Gavin didn't say anything about that. Was that when he was in Florida?"

Larry nodded. "Josh was starting to make a name for himself. With a little celebrity, the weirdos come out of the woodwork. Gavin saved my son's bacon more than once. I am so glad he was there on the day Josh was shot. Things could have been a lot worse if he hadn't been."

"What happened?"

The older man rested a gnarled hand on the back of the chair. He shook his head. "A delusional male fan with a gun who thought Josh should respond to his overtures to go into business together."

"And your son?"

"He's alive, thanks to Gavin." The man picked up another picture. "You have to revise your dreams and make career changes all the time. I started out thinking I was going to manage a gas station for the rest of my life. Didn't think real estate would be the thing that put me over the top." He showed the picture to Julia. "That's my new grandson that Josh and Cecelia finally got around to making for me. He was always too busy racing to think about a family."

"So he's not a race-car driver anymore?"

"No, he had quite a bit of money in the bank from racing, so he bought himself a hotel. He and Cecelia run it together, and Josh stays put instead of traveling all over the world."

Julia took a bite of her cinnamon roll and wandered over to a window. Outside, Gavin walked along the shoreline with long, deliberate steps. "Gavin is a very good bodyguard."

Larry crossed the room and stood beside her. "I thought that boy would have settled down by now.

'Course, the kind of women you meet in his line of work usually aren't the kind you marry, all Richie-rich and spoiled."

Larry had a humorous way of looking at things. "Aren't you kind of Richie-rich?" Julia teased.

"By my bank account. But let's face it, you can take the hillbilly out of the hills and put him in a fancy house, but he's still a hillbilly. Can't bring myself to throw much away, got to try and fix everything with duct tape."

Julia threw back her head and laughed. Then she turned a half circle around the room, admiring the nice furniture. "So this is all kind of a pretense."

"Pretty much." He looked back out at Gavin and shook his head, lost in thought. "Just thought that boy would have found someone by now."

After Larry slipped away to the kitchen saying something about finding some honey for his tea, Julia watched Gavin through the window. He had shoved his hands into the pockets of his coat, and his head was down, as though he were thinking deeply about something.

She found herself longing to reach out to him, to comfort him in whatever it was that was upsetting him.

SEVENTEEN

"Good news." Gavin made his way down the rock path to where Julia sat enjoying her early morning cup of coffee.

He'd stepped away from her to take the phone call that had come in. Out of habit, he had kept her in his line of sight. After several days on the island without incident, he had found himself relaxing for the first time since he had taken the assignment to guard Julia. They were safe here.

Julia looked over the steaming mug she had cradled in her hands. "What happened?"

"The guy who attacked you back at Elizabeth's has started to sing. Elijah has a stepbrother who works in the kitchen at the prison." He could never totally let his guard down, but this victory made him even more confident that the threat against Julia had lessened.

"So they fired the guy?"

Gavin nodded. "Elijah can't receive any visitors. There is no way he can communicate with his followers."

Julia rose to her feet. "You seem happier than I've ever seen you."

"We're going to get you to that trial, Julia. The end

is in sight." Though this recent development lifted a weight off him, he had mixed feelings about the trial. Yes, he wanted Elijah put away for good. Yes, he wanted Julia to feel safe and have her freedom back. But once the trial was over, Julia would be getting on with her life, and he would no longer be a part of it—unless he could tell her his feelings before then.

"Yes," she said. "The end is in sight." A sadness seemed to flicker across her eyes, but then he thought he was reading too much into a passing change in her expression.

"I'll make arrangements for the lawyers to come here to the island to finish the preparation. We should be able to pull things together in the next couple of days."

Larry came down the hill toward them. "How are you kids doing this morning?"

Julia took a sip of her coffee. "I slept better the last couple of nights than I've slept in a long time."

"I think both of us have had the dark circles disappear from under our eyes," Gavin added.

"The island does that for you." Larry peered out at the lake. "The water's calm this morning. The two of you should take a boat out. You can take the canoe if you don't want to listen to the motor the whole time."

Gavin tensed. He felt safe on the island, but there was no need to get sloppy. "Are there houses along the shoreline or on other islands?"

"I'll show you on the map where you can go to avoid that sort of thing. You're not likely to find people out on the water for a pleasure cruise this time of year, either. This is the first calm day we've had in a while. Just thought you two might like to get out on the water."

"I like the idea." Julia bounced on her feet, toe to heel. "Could we go, Gavin?"

The pleading in her eyes tugged at his heart. She'd been so confined for so long. They weren't in a dangerous place. This wasn't the department store or the hot springs. "A boat ride sounds like a good idea. I just need to make the arrangement to get your lawyers here, then we can go."

He liked the sparkle he saw in Julia's eyes.

She turned to face Larry. "I'm good at reading maps. Maybe while Gavin's making his calls, you can show me the best place to go."

Two hours later, Julia showed up at his door with a picnic basket in one hand and map in the other. "All done with your calls?"

A vitality seemed to have returned to her demeanor. The wild red hair only added to the effect.

He snapped his phone shut. "The Flemings will be here tomorrow. They will take extreme precaution to get here." He reached out his hand for the picnic basket. "Here, let me take that." Their fingers touched briefly, and warmth spread through his fingertips and up his arm. Being in a place where they could both relax a little had only confirmed his love for her.

Larry came with them as they made their way down to the boat. After Julia and Gavin got in the boat, he pushed them off. He waved and shouted, "If you are not back in a few hours, I'll come out looking for you." He pointed to the motorboat in the dock. "Cell phones usually work okay."

Gavin and Julia paddled out to the open water. Once they were in a place where the shoreline was distant and indistinct, they stopped to rest. "We can just drift for a while and enjoy the quiet."

She tilted her head and watched the sky. "Pretty out here, isn't it? So peaceful." Her lip quivered, and she put a palm to her chest. "It takes my breath away." Her voice stirred with emotion.

Gavin took in the expression of serenity on Julia's face. What was she thinking, this beautiful woman? "Does it give you hope?"

She lifted her chin in a slow nod. "Yes. There will come a time when no walls can hold me in." She turned slightly in the boat, taking in her surroundings. "I have enough faith to believe that now."

He scooted toward her. "You have more than enough faith. I always thought you did."

She opened the picnic basket and handed him a sandwich. "I know this is kind of silly, but going out for a picnic like this feels like…almost a date."

Her comment took him by surprise. "A date?"

Her cheeks flushed with color, and she scooted back in the boat. "I didn't mean a real date—I mean, I'm not delusional. I know we aren't *really* on a date."

He moved closer to her. "I know you're not delusional." As flustered as she was, she had never looked so beautiful.

"They took me when I was thirteen, Gavin. I've never even been on a date. I know the picnic isn't intended to be a real date. I guess I just wanted something that felt like I was getting the pieces of my life back." She waved her hand in the air. "I know I'm not making any sense."

Her mile-a-minute banter was endearing. So she was imagining the two of them on a date. The idea of a date with her appealed to him. She stared at him with wide, blue eyes. Her lips parted. Everything about her appealed to him. He leaned toward her, covering her mouth with his. Aware that this was probably her first kiss, he brushed his lips gently over hers and then touched his thumb to her mouth. "You're making perfect sense."

Julia drew back, stunned and breathless. "I kept thinking you just thought I was a job."

"That's never what I thought." This time, he gathered her in his arms. She responded by leaning closer. Her cool, smooth hand skimmed over his neck, and he kissed her again, pressing harder. Surrounded by that sweet citrus scent, holding her close enough to relish the warmth of her made every worry he had about the future more bearable. He kissed her again.

The promise he'd made to her father rose to the surface of his awareness. He pulled back. "I'm sorry. I shouldn't have done that."

Disappointment clouded her expression. "What are you talking about?"

He gathered her hands in his. "No, I didn't mean the kiss. I've been wanting to do that for a long time. It's just that I made a promise to your father that I wouldn't see you romantically."

She let out a gasp of air. "What? I'm old enough to make that decision myself."

"That promise was easy enough to make before I got to know you."

"What exactly did my father say to you?" She could not hide her irritation.

"He thought you were still fragile psychologically, but I can see that is not true after all we've been through together. You are stronger and more grounded than any woman I've ever met."

She continued to shake her head. "Why would he say something like that?"

"Julia, he is only trying to protect you. He lost you once. I am sure he feels enormous guilt that he didn't somehow prevent the abduction. He's probably afraid of losing you again, so he's overprotective. All that has happened, plus the guilt, messes with his perception of you."

"I hadn't thought if it that way. I know my father loves me. But it's like I'm still thirteen to him because he missed out on all that." Julia sat back in the boat and crossed her arms. "I wish he could see me the way you see me."

"He will in time. I think it's important to earn his respect by keeping my promise. Then maybe it will open the door for me to talk to him about us."

She bent her head and looked up at him coyly. "I guess this means no more kisses?"

His thumb grazed her cheek. "You have no idea how much I want to kiss you again."

A faint smile illuminated her whole face. "Me, too, but you're right. I'd like my father's blessing in this."

The afterglow of the kiss made his head buzz. "How about that picnic?"

Julia took more of the supplies out. They ate with the water lapping against the boat as it swayed on the waves.

As they talked, he realized it was a gift just to be in her presence, enjoying her company.

She took a bite of her sandwich. "Do you think Larry will notice something different when we get back?"

Gavin shook his head. "I think he planned for this to happen while we were out on the boat."

Julia tilted her head. "He must have noticed something about the way we interacted. I had a nice talk with him yesterday. He's so grateful that you were with his son when he was shot."

Gavin sat back in the boat. "That's what he said?"

He hadn't intended for his voice to grow cold. The defensiveness happened automatically.

She grabbed his hand and pulled him toward her. "Hey, I don't know exactly what happened in Florida, but it seems like your view of events is different from Larry's." She squeezed his hands, refusing to let go.

Gavin's hands curled into fists within hers. "My decisions led to Joshua being shot. I should have been able to prevent it. Maybe Larry is okay with how things turned out, but I'm sure Joshua blames me."

"How do you know that? Have you talked to him?"

"Why wouldn't he? He depended on me to protect him." Gavin massaged his chest where it had grown tight. He'd carried this burden alone for so long. This was the first time he had talked about it to anyone. "I let him down."

"And maybe if you hadn't been there at all, he would have been dead." She looked him in the eyes. The intensity of her gaze told him he could not look away. "I was eaten up with guilt by Marlena's death. A very wise person pointed out that I did the best I could when a split-second decision needed to be made. Maybe that very wise person needs to take his own advice."

He scooted to the other side of the boat as her words sank in. "I prayed that God would take the guilt away. Maybe it hasn't gone away because I deserve to feel guilty." He rested his head in his hands.

"God doesn't operate that way." She took a breath and spoke slowly. "You need to forgive *yourself* for what happened."

He wrestled with her words, not wanting to receive them. "Forgive myself?" Her wisdom, the depth of her understanding and her willingness to gently push him to the place where he had to face what he had been running from made him love her even more.

She nodded. "And then I think you need to call Joshua. His father doesn't blame you. Joshua might have the same perspective."

And he might not. Gavin tensed. All the same, it was a phone call he knew he would have to make. He needed to at least make an effort toward repairing the relationship.

He stared at the wise woman in front of him. A single snowflake hit Julia's face, melted and trickled down her cheek. Several more landed on her hair. He leaned toward her and wiped it away with his finger as he stared into her eyes. He tilted his head and stared at the darkening clouds. "Storm's moving in. So much for a calm day. I suppose we better head back." They paddled together, creating a steady rhythm as they worked in tandem.

By the time he steered the boat into the dock, the snow was falling steadily. His boots were tall enough that the cold water didn't seep in when he stepped into the shallow water. He reached out for Julia, gathering her into his arms and carrying her the few steps it took to get her to the dry shore.

On the way back to the house, though they didn't hold hands, they walked close enough so their hands brushed against each other. Each look from her, every time she touched him—intentionally or by accident—made his feet melt in his shoes.

His world had shifted 180 degrees. The barriers between him and Julia were gone.

As Larry's house came into view, he realized that

even though the end was in sight and he and Julia were in a good place, they faced an uphill battle in more ways than one.

EIGHTEEN

After breakfast the next morning, Julia found Gavin in the study. "We've got time for you to make that phone call to Joshua before the Flemings come to do the trial prep."

Gavin set the magazine he'd been flipping through on a side table. He massaged the back of his neck where his muscles had instantly knotted up at the thought of talking to his childhood friend. "Guess I've put it off long enough."

She nodded. "I'll stay with you if you like."

He scooted over on the couch and pulled his phone out. Julia sat beside him. She had shown such courage with way more than a difficult phone call. He studied the phone for a moment.

"What are you thinking?"

He leaned toward her so their shoulders touched. "I was just thinking that you inspire me to face the hard things in life."

She pressed her lips together. "Thank you."

He dialed the number and waited. He heard Joshua's greeting on the other end of the line and braced himself by saying a quick prayer. Julia slipped her hand into his.

He swallowed. "Hey, Joshua."

"Gavin? What took you so long, man?"

"I know I should have gotten in touch sooner." The warm reception from his friend was encouraging. "I just…I had a hard time seeing you in that hospital bed. Guess I ran away."

Joshua didn't answer immediately. When he did talk, something about his tone changed. "I had a hard time seeing me in that hospital bed."

As the tension spread through him, Gavin pressed the phone harder against his ear. "I know it wasn't easy. I kept replaying that moment in my mind. If only I had registered that guy's face faster. If only I had pushed you out of the way faster. If only I had pushed you in a different direction."

"Hey, man, you did what you knew to do. I couldn't ask for anything more."

Joshua's words seemed genuine. He didn't blame Gavin. Why, then, did he detect an undercurrent of anger.

Gavin closed his eyes and tilted his head. "I'm so sorry you can't race anymore."

"I won't lie to you. The adjustment was hard, and I was angry at everyone for a while. So in a way, it's better that you didn't stick around. I would have said things I regretted, but I'm doing okay. I'm a dad now." Again, Joshua paused. "You want to know what I'm really mad about?"

Gavin took in a sharp breath. "Yeah. Tell me."

Julia squeezed his hand a little tighter.

"I understand you had to leave and sort through things. I know that's how you are. I'm glad you did. I needed time, too."

"Are you still angry?" Gavin prepared himself for the answer, whatever it might be.

"I'm not angry about the shooting anymore. I'm mad that it took you so long to call. I missed you."

Gavin let out a sigh of relief as affection for his friend welled up. "Well, I suppose I'll just have to come down to Florida and whip you into shape."

"We're coming up there sooner or later. Why don't you make a plan to come over to Dad's place, and then you can whip me into shape."

"I can do that." The two men said their goodbyes and Gavin hung up. He wrapped his arms around Julia and held her tight as joy burst through him. "Thank you."

She rested her head on his shoulder.

He buried his face in her hair, enjoying the softness of it. "We're almost there, aren't we?"

"Almost," she said. "This trial isn't going to be easy. I can't lie to you. When I think about facing Elijah in the courtroom, I'm afraid."

He placed his hand on her neck. "I'll be there with you."

Julia's fears were not misplaced. This last hurdle, facing Elijah, was the biggest. He had concerns, too, that the followers might try to get at Julia while she was en route to the courtroom, or even once the trial began. The followers weren't going to give up easily.

Julia stood in front of the large windows of the house looking out toward the dock. The Flemings were late. Anxiety coiled through her stomach. She'd awakened this morning ready to face the final step in getting ready for this trial.

She checked her watch for the tenth time.

Gavin stepped into the room. "Are they here yet?" she asked.

He shook his head.

Gavin then placed his hands on his hips. His open jacket revealed the gun he had borrowed from Larry. He had relaxed some since they had come here, and Elijah could no longer give orders from his jail cell, but Gavin never totally let his guard down.

He placed a supportive hand on her shoulder. "I spoke to them less than forty-five minutes ago. They will be here. They're renting a boat and coming from a dock that is nowhere near where Larry picked us up."

His touch caused a surge of heat through her. She turned away. Looking into his eyes only made her want another kiss from him. The sooner the trial was over, the sooner they could talk to her father. Getting through the trial prep was one more thing she could check off her list in the steps toward freedom…and maybe being able to be with Gavin.

She rubbed her arms. A chill had come into the house since she'd let the fire die out. "Who were you talking to on the phone?"

"Elizabeth called. Lydia turned herself in."

A sense of elation spread through her. "That's good news."

"Police will probably want to charge her for helping Elijah's men. She's underage, so it shouldn't be too bad."

She caught herself, not wanting to ask the next question. "Did she want to go back to the compound?"

"Elizabeth said she seemed open to the idea of some sort of protective custody. She'll get the psychological help she needs."

"I hope things work out for her." Maybe somewhere

down the road, she could see Lydia again and help her with adjusting to life outside the cult.

Gavin's phone rang again, and he stepped to one side. A smile spread across his face. "Joshua, what's up?"

Since Gavin had made the first phone call to Joshua, the relationship seemed to be mending. They were talking quite a bit.

Julia stepped away from the window. Staring out it wasn't going to make them come any sooner. She sat down on a couch and clicked on the television, tapping her fingers on the arm of the sofa.

She watched the end of a mindless sitcom while Gavin joked with his friend. Gavin stepped into the hallway to continue his conversation above the sound of the television.

"I can turn it off," Julia offered.

He covered the phone. "It's okay. Watch it if it gets your mind off waiting."

She noticed that he stood at an angle so he could still see her. His vigilance never subsided. A teaser for the local news came on after the sitcom credits ran.

Julia glanced out the window. A boat neared the dock. Gavin was still engrossed in his conversation. Filled with anticipation, she jumped up, grabbed her coat and headed out the door just as the local news came on.

Gavin heard the door slam shut.

"Hang on, Julia. I'm right behind you." He spoke into the phone. "Joshua, I gotta go."

He slipped his phone into a coat pocket. The voice of the female reporter on the television caught his attention.

The world seemed to move in slow motion as the

dark-haired reporter looked into the camera and said, "Our lead story tonight is that there has been a jail break in Thornburg, Montana. The cult leader who calls himself Elijah True escaped. Guards didn't realize Mr. True was gone until evening check-in. Mr. True may have had help from the outside, since initial investigation indicates that he did not flee on foot. He may be armed and is considered dangerous."

Gavin turned toward the window. Adrenaline pumped through his system. Julia stood on the edge of the dock. The boat neared the shore. Her enthusiastic waving stopped. A man burst out from beneath a tarp.

Gavin pushed through the door and ran down the stone walkway.

Elijah had grabbed Julia and shoved Victoria Fleming out of the boat. Gavin moved down the stone steps at a breakneck pace as he pulled his weapon and shouted. "Don't you dare take her!" He raised his gun and aimed.

Elijah shoved Julia into the boat and sped off.

Victoria Fleming stumbled to her feet, stepping into the line of fire. Gavin lowered his gun and raced to the shore as the boat drew farther away from the shore.

"Where is your husband?"

"Back at the dock." Victoria was out of breath. She touched her palm to her chest and shook her head, as though she could not accept the violence that had just occurred. "He knocked Roy unconscious. We took precautions like you said. The followers must have been watching our office for days, just waiting."

Gavin jumped into Larry's boat and yanked on the pull cord. "Notify the police." The boat revved to life, and he steered it clear of the dock.

Elijah's boat was still in view, but wouldn't be once

he rounded the bend. He couldn't push the boat to go any faster. He couldn't see Julia. Elijah must have made her lie down in the boat. Steering the boat with one hand, he aimed his pistol.

The shot went wild. He had to get closer.

Elijah's boat slowed then wove erratically through the water when he reached down and picked up a rifle. Gavin thought he saw Julia's red head.

Gavin dove for the deck of the boat as Elijah fired the rifle. Pain seared through him, and he knew he'd been shot.

NINETEEN

Elijah shouted at Julia, "Get up and steer this thing!" The venom in his voice made her recoil.

When she grabbed the steering wheel and looked above the rim of the boat, she saw Gavin following them in the second boat only for a moment before a shot zinged through the air. Gavin gripped his shoulder and fell forward in the boat.

Invisible weight that made it hard to breathe pressed on her. Gavin was shot.

Elijah yanked on Julia's red hair.

"Now, you and I have some talking to do, angel face." He pried her hand off the steering wheel.

Rage as she had never before experienced coursed through her.

Elijah waggled a finger at her and pulled a small pistol out of a jacket pocket. "Don't go getting any ideas."

She lunged at him. He pushed her to the floor of the boat. The pain in her back immobilized her. He scrambled so he loomed over her, waving the pistol in her face. "You do what I say. You hear me?"

Though she nodded and feigned surrender, inwardly her heart rebelled.

No, Elijah, I will not do what you say, not ever again.

"Now stay down," Elijah barked. He backed off and returned to steering the boat. He held the pistol in such a way that she knew he would fire it if she moved.

Julia resisted the desire to sit up to see where Gavin was. She had no way of knowing how badly he'd been shot. All she needed was the right opportunity, and she could get away from this man.

Diving off the boat into the freezing cold water would mean certain death. Hopefully he intended to take her to dry land before he shot her. She had more of a chance of escape that way.

She saw the intent to murder in his stone-cold eyes. His mind had become so distorted by the desire for revenge, so unable to process his idea that she had betrayed him, that the consequences of shooting her didn't even register with him. She was a threat to him, someone who would topple his house of cards. His world where he had all the control. He wanted her dead.

She knew, too, that trying to reason with him would only make him angry.

Without moving her head, her gaze traveled to the rifle that lay on the bottom of the boat. Elijah had been a strong man, but months in jail had made him thinner and probably weaker. Did she have the strength to hit him hard enough to land him in the water? Then she could speed away in the boat to help Gavin.

She thought better of it. If she didn't succeed, he'd shoot her on the spot. Maybe she could distract him. "How did you get out of jail?"

"My men set it up on their own since I couldn't get messages to them anymore." He looked at her with wild eyes, his voice filled with rage. "Because they are loyal no matter what." He spat the words out.

A chill ran down Julia's back.

He slowed the boat. She didn't dare turn around to see if they were approaching land. She lay frozen, watching him. She'd only get one chance for escape. It would have to be the right chance.

The boat swayed as he killed the engine. He grabbed the rifle and jumped to shore. "Now, come on." In this light, his eyes looked yellow and they tore through her like a machete.

She was shaken, afraid even, but something had changed since her last encounter with him when he had killed Marlena. An inner calm lay just beneath her fear.

He grabbed her shirt at the collar and pulled her close. "I'll teach you to file charges against me. You and your big mouth have destroyed everything the True Church worked for."

He pushed her forward through the trees. "Put your hands on the back of your head."

As she stumbled forward, she heard him rack a bullet into the chamber of the rifle. Her heart raced. She scanned the area around her, but found no means of escape. Despair set in. Maybe this was it. She wouldn't be able to get away. Images of Gavin plagued her. Was he lying bleeding in that boat? Was he alive?

They came to a clearing with a flat rock in the middle of it.

"Now sit down," he said.

She sat on the rock and looked up at Elijah, expecting to see him take aim at her. Instead, the rifle dropped to his thigh, and he turned so she saw him in profile.

Though she had intended to ask him what he was going to do, she could only let out a gurgle.

He checked his watch.

The revelation spread through her slowly. Hope returned. He was waiting for somebody.

"Why not just kill me now?"

"And have your blood on my hands? No, thanks. I've been in jail enough." He offered her a grin that sent chills over her skin. "I've got plenty of loyal followers who will take care of that for me."

"And then what? They'll still link you to me. You escaped from jail. You will be punished for what you did to Marlena."

"You think." He leaned close. "The True Church has quite a stash of cash. They won't find me in South America."

Through the trees, she heard the hum of a car engine. Elijah must have taken her back to the mainland. She turned in the direction of the noise.

Elijah put the butt of the rifle against her cheek and pushed. "You don't need to be looking around."

The motor of the car stopped, and she heard the cacophony of men's voices coming through the trees from down the hill. She could separate out at least two, maybe three male voices.

"Do they know that you're going to steal everything from them and abandon them?"

Elijah's face turned crimson. "That's not what I'm doing. I'm their leader, it is important that I be kept alive and free."

Three men came into the clearing.

Julia jumped to her feet. She was outmanned and outgunned. The only hope she had was to turn them on each other. She pointed at Elijah. "He intends to liquidate all the church assets and escape to South America."

The men looked from Elijah and then to Julia.

"You're a liar," said one of the men. "Elijah wouldn't do that."

"That's right." Elijah stuck his chest out, but his voice gave away his fear. "I'll set up down in Chile, and the rest of you can meet me there."

One of the men adjusted his grip on the knife he held. "You didn't say anything about setting up in Chile. You just said we needed to start over."

It didn't look as though any of the other men had come with guns.

"Look, just take the girl and deal with her." Elijah managed the commanding don't-argue-with-me voice that she was so familiar with. He pulled the pistol out of his pocket, ready to hand it to one of them. "Let's just stick with the plan."

The men looked at each other. Julia took advantage of the momentary distraction and doubt when everyone's guard was down. She lunged forward and grabbed the rifle. She pulled the trigger without aiming. Elijah yelped and doubled over.

She didn't stay to see how badly he was hurt. She broke through the trees and ran in the direction she thought the shore was. Behind her, she could hear Elijah screaming. His threats tore through her like bullets.

No matter what, she was not going to let this man win. She pushed branches out of the way. Elijah's voice grew closer, angrier.

The trees thinned. Julia stumbled forward. She fell on the wet sand of the shoreline. Her muscles reverberated from the impact. She heard Elijah roar behind her and then felt a boot on her back, pressing her into the rocky shore. She gasped for air.

"Back off from her."

Gavin's clear voice broke through her pain and fear. She could see his feet as he made his way up the shore-line. Blood dripped on the sand. She lifted her head. Blood stained his right shoulder.

"I suppose you're going to make me!" Elijah shouted.

Gavin lifted his pistol with his good arm and aimed. "Yeah, I'm going to make you." Despite his injury, his voice was strong, authoritative.

The weight of Elijah's boot on her back vaporized. When Julia flipped over, Elijah was kneeling sideways on the ground. His foot was bleeding where she had shot him.

One of the followers came through the trees, but stopped short and threw up his arms when he saw Gavin.

Elijah's face distorted with pain as he bent over. He made a high-pitched, child-like sound. She saw him for what he was. A small, weak man who was all bluster and no real courage.

"You all right?" Gavin's hand brushed over her hair.

Julia nodded and rose to her feet. With his wounded arm, he pushed her behind him.

"There are two more men in the trees just off that road."

"Victoria has called the police. They should be here any minute. These guys aren't going anywhere."

The sound of a boat engine caused her to turn. Two men whose brown uniforms indicated they were law-enforcement officers approached the beach.

Julia came around to stand beside Gavin. The grimace on his face indicated that he was in pain, yet he did not allow the gun in his hand to waver.

The two officers moved quickly up the shoreline and took Elijah and the other man into custody.

"Two more of them are in the trees." Julia pointed.

One of the officers took off running with his weapon drawn. Julia drew her attention to Gavin's bloodstained shirt.

"It just grazed the shoulder. I'll be all right."

She placed her hand on the hard muscle just above the wound. "I'm glad you came when you did."

"Looked like you were doing just fine. He wasn't going to get far with that wound to his foot. I could tell he was losing strength."

"We should get you to the hospital. I'll drive." After they talked to the police, Julia waited while Gavin got in the boat. She jumped in and started the motor.

Gavin grew paler as they got farther away from the shore. He leaned forward and gripped her shoulder. "You've got that worried look on your face, Julia."

She shivered when she saw the size of the bloodstain on his shirt. "First priority is to get you to a doctor."

He moved toward her and grabbed her hand. "I'm doing okay." He brushed his hand over her cheek. "When he took you, I was so afraid I'd lost you forever."

A lump formed in her throat. "I saw you go down in that boat, and I…" It wasn't just that they had grown used to each other because they had been so close for the last month. Her feelings weren't a byproduct of all the danger they had to live with. The truth was, she couldn't imagine life without him. When she had thought she'd lost him, all hope had faded.

He pressed his forehead against hers. "I know the feeling. It won't be long now, Julia. We just need to get through this trial."

TWENTY

On the day Julia was to take the stand, the courtroom was packed. It killed Gavin not to be able to be with her once the trial started. He was assured that for the course of the trial, the state would provide security, but none of that soothed him. He wanted to be the one protecting her.

He sat next to Julia's father, William, and Elizabeth sat on the other side of him.

"The state wishes to call Julia Randel."

A side door to the courtroom opened and Julia appeared, escorted by an officer of the court. Gavin leaned forward in his seat. Julia maintained a neutral expression as she looked around the courtroom.

Because so much time had been lost, the Flemings had spent the last few days drilling Julia. Gavin had been able to be there with her through all that. He thought she was holding up pretty well, but he hadn't seen her for two days. Julia lifted her chin, scanning the courtroom. He tilted his head when she saw him. She squared her shoulders, seeming to gather strength from having made eye contact with him.

William leaned toward Gavin. "She looks tired."

"She'll be all right," whispered Elizabeth.

Victoria Fleming began her questioning. Julia answered all of the questions with poise.

"Your witness." Victoria sat down and the defense attorney rose to his feet, buttoning his suit jacket. He rubbed his chin, studied Julia and then looked back over at Elijah, which caused everyone in the courtroom to crane their necks toward Elijah.

Elijah was clean shaven and dressed like a business man. None of the anger was evident in his demeanor, and his eyes no longer held the crazed look that Gavin had seen the day he was taken into custody. The man was an actor of the highest quality.

As the defense attorney approached Julia, William braced his hand on the bench in front of him. "I wish she didn't have to go through this."

Elijah's attorney rested his hand on the stand and leaned toward Julia.

Julia flinched.

"Ms. Randel, can you state your relationship to the accused?"

"Elijah True kidnapped me when I was thirteen."

As expected, the lawyer drilled Julia about why she stayed in the cult for seven years. Julia held her ground, answering the questions in a strong, clear voice.

Gavin leaned toward William. "The only option here is to make Julia look like an unreliable witness. He's going to do everything to try to shake her apart."

The lawyer patted his stomach and then said, "Let's move on to the night of the murder. After seven years, you chose the night of Marlena Kenyon's death to run away. Is that correct?"

Julia's face blanched, but she answered the question without her voice faltering. "I didn't choose it. My escape wasn't planned."

The lawyer walked away from the witness stand, obviously pausing for dramatic effect. "So your good friend was dying, and instead of staying with her, you decided to run away?"

Elijah inched forward in his chair. The scraping sound of the legs moving across the floor was like fingernails on a chalkboard. Elijah cleared his throat and looked toward Julia.

Gavin tensed.

Come on, Julia, you can do this.

Julia narrowed her eyes at Elijah and then looked back toward the attorney. She folded her hands in her lap and sat up straighter. "I didn't check for a pulse, but I knew she was dead. Elijah was already stirring up people against me. I was afraid for my life. I wish I could have stayed with her, but I had to make a split-second decision and I did the best I knew how to do in that moment."

Gavin watched William's demeanor visibly change as he stared at his daughter.

He leaned toward the older man. "She is stronger than you know."

Stunned, William nodded. "I can see that."

The defense attorney asked more questions about the murder, drawing out the details. Julia remained in control.

"No further questions, your honor." The defense attorney was adept at not giving anything away with his body language as he moved back toward his client.

Julia was dismissed once Roy Fleming said he had no further questions. The officer escorted her out of the room through a side door.

Emptiness invaded Gavin's consciousness as the

door closed behind her. Would he be able to be with her before the verdict was read?

The judge gave the jury instructions before dismissing them to come back with a verdict and declaring a recess. People slowly got up and trailed out into the hallway. Elizabeth excused herself.

William Randel pressed his back against the bench and stared at the ceiling. "I think they will get a conviction, don't you?"

"Julia did a good job. The Flemings showed that the testimony from other cult members was contradictory and driven by loyalty to Elijah, not the truth." Gavin shifted in his seat and took a breath. He wanted William's blessing if he and Julia were going to have any kind of a life together. Now was the time to ask. "Your daughter is a strong, capable woman."

William sat up straighter and looked at Gavin. "I do think she has come a long way since her escape. Two years ago, she wouldn't have been able to stand up to Elijah like that."

"She has been through so much this past month. With each incident, I saw how clear-headed and courageous she was."

William nodded. "Is there something you want to say to me?"

Gavin braced himself. "I owe you an apology. I broke my promise. You asked me not to see Julia romantically—"

William's expression hardened. "What have you done?"

"My only desire is to protect your daughter…in every way. And if I thought she wasn't emotionally ready, I never would have even entertained the thought, but I have fallen in love with your daughter."

William Randel clasped his gnarled hands together and stared at them. "When I saw her on that stand, her strength was so unexpected. If you could have seen her in the first few months after she was home…"

"I know that the wounds will never totally go away for Julia, but I would like to be there for her. I would like to be a part of her life."

William shook his head as his resistance built. "But you have only known her a month."

The immense loss both Julia and her father had endured pierced his heart. "I know that you and she have some catching up to do, and if you don't want me in the picture, I'll walk away."

"I don't hold it against you for breaking your promise. She is not the frightened child who came back to me. I see that now, but please, I need time."

William's words felt like a blow to his stomach. The bottom dropped out of Gavin's world. He couldn't fathom a life without Julia, but he had to respect her father's wishes. "I understand. If you ever feel ready to let me into Julia's life…"

A realization spread across William's face. "If I feel ready?"

"Yes." Gavin nodded, uncertain of what William was thinking, as his stomach turned in knots.

William shook his head. "I guess it can't always be about me. I missed out on her adolescence, but I don't want to rob her of her future because I'm trying to get that back."

Gavin sat back in his seat as an overwhelming sense of joy spread through him.

William patted his shoulder. "You should go find her. I'm sure it's going to be a while before the jury comes back."

Gavin rose up from his chair and skirted through the crowd out into the hallway. He had no idea where the witnesses went once they were done testifying.

The officer who had escorted Julia into the courtroom stood in the hallway drinking something from a Styrofoam cup.

He looked up as Gavin approached him. "Sir?"

"Can you tell me where the witnesses are taken after they testify?"

The officer eyed Gavin suspiciously. "Can I ask why?"

"I'm looking for Julia Randel. I'm her bodyguard." *And I want to spend the rest of my life with her.*

The man studied him a moment longer and then pointed toward the stairs that lead down to large glass doors. "She headed straight outside, said something about feeling the sun on her face. An officer went with her. She's under police protection until the trial is over."

Gavin's heartbeat hiccupped over concern for Julia's safety. He didn't trust anyone but himself to protect her. Elijah was still in custody. All the evidence pointed to the followers losing the will to fight. Those who had been caught had attempted-murder charges filed against them. He doubted any others wanted that kind of legal action against them, but all it took was one zealot who didn't care if he lived or died.

Gavin made his way down the stairs and pushed the door open, scanning the area around the courthouse. He felt a sense of urgency and a strong desire to be with Julia as he made his way across the street to a small park.

He found her sitting on a bench behind a clump of evergreens. The police officer stood about twenty feet from her. As he raced toward her, he realized that maybe he had been foolhardy. Maybe all of her feelings of affection had risen up because of the stress they were under. She might have decided to get on with her life, attend college and leave any reminder of Elijah and the trial in the past.

She looked serene with her head tilted back and her eyes closed.

He hesitated in his step as he approached her.

Julia relished the warmth of the sun on her skin. This is what she had waited for. This sense of freedom. Confident the jury would find Elijah guilty, she contemplated her future. She wanted to go to college to study psychology. Maybe then, she could counsel other young women like Lydia.

She heard footsteps and opened her eyes. The officer moved in. His hand wavered over his gun.

Julia held up a hand. "It's all right, officer." She smiled at Gavin. "I know this man."

Her breath caught in her throat. Gavin stood in front of her. He looked appealing in his camel coat and leather gloves.

"Have you heard yet? Have they come back with a verdict?"

He shook his head. His expression held an earnest quality.

"What is it then?" Tension twisted through her.

He held his arms open for her. "I have your father's blessing for us to be together."

She rose to her feet, trying to fathom what a future with Gavin would look like. "So did you decide to get out of the bodyguard business?"

He shook his head. "It's what I do. It's who I am." He

reached out and brushed his hand over her cheek. "A really pretty lady had belief in my ability when I didn't believe it myself. She restored my confidence."

She closed the distance between them. "How about that. I know a really handsome man who saw me as strong and capable when no one else did."

"Hmm...maybe those two people should get together." He wrapped an arm around her waist and pulled her toward him, leaning down to kiss her.

She relished the safety of his arms as his lips covered hers. She pulled back and looked up into his brown eyes. "Maybe they should."

"I know we've only known each other for a month, so I am willing to take this slow."

"How slow?"

"How about the rest of our lives?"

"Deal." She wrapped her arms around his neck. The sunshine and the sense of freedom that she had were wonderful and precious. But none of it compared to being in Gavin Shane's tender embrace.

EPILOGUE

"You look beautiful," Elizabeth gathered Julia into a sideways hug as she came out of Larry's house and looked down the stone walkway that led to the shoreline of his island. Her father stood at the base of the stairs waiting to walk her to where Gavin and his best man, Joshua, stood. Everyone who mattered to her was here.

Julia stared down at the cream-colored satin of her wedding dress. "Thank you."

The green trees and purple-and-white flowers that colored the hillside made a perfect backdrop for a wedding. A big contrast from the stark winter landscape of a year-and-a-half ago when she had lived in fear for her life. All of that was behind her now. Elijah was in prison. His followers had disbanded.

Elizabeth gave her another hug. "This is the perfect place for a wedding."

"And the hot springs is the perfect place for a honeymoon. Thanks for offering it to me and Gavin."

Elizabeth adjusted the comb in Julia's blond hair. "Your father's waiting. You'd better get going."

And Gavin was waiting. Julia lifted the skirt of her dress and made her way down the stone steps. Her father held his arm out for her to take it. Gavin turned to gaze at her. As she walked toward him, she realized that God had more than restored all that was taken from her.

* * * * *

Dear Reader,

Through tragic circumstances, Julia has lost a huge part of her growing-up years. She missed out on ordinary things like learning to drive, graduation and going to prom—all the milestones that happen for most people. Julia longed to do such mundane activities as walking outside and sitting in a coffee shop. While most of us might desire a life of adventure, Julia looked forward to the day when normal would happen.

As I was writing this book, I thought about what a gift ordinary things like a morning cup of coffee or feeling safe in my own home are. Prayers of thanks come easily for the extraordinary things that God does in our lives—curing an illness or getting us through a hard relationship or providing in tough financial times. Writing this book has prompted me to be more thankful for the parts of my life that are just there automatically, from the abundance of groceries in the store and books on my library shelf to the sound of the rain through my open window. All of these are gifts from God, worth thanking Him for.

Blessings,

Sharon

Questions for Discussion

1. To get through her difficult month before the trial, Julia often imagined what her life would be like after the trial was over. Have you ever had to endure a difficult situation? What gave you hope that things would change?

2. What memories did Julia have of her mother? Why was Marlena's death doubly hard for Julia?

3. What deliberate things did Julia do to cope while Elijah held her captive?

4. What was the most exciting part of the book for you?

5. Do you think you could deal with the kind of confinement and isolation Julia had to live through after her escape?

6. In what ways did Julia help Gavin gain his confidence back as a bodyguard?

7. What do you think Elizabeth's role was in the story? In what ways was she helpful, and in what ways was she hurtful?

8. In a moment of crisis Julia, recalled a Bible verse, "I can do all things through Christ, who strengthens me" (Phlippians 4:13). Has a verse ever come into your mind at the moment you needed it? Did

you ever memorize a Bible verse to help get you through a hard situation?

9. Why was Julia's father so protective of her? Did you agree or disagree with his choices?

10. Do you think Gavin showed respect toward Julia's father? In what way?

11. Like Julia and Gavin, all of us have had parts of our lives that we wish we could undo. Sometimes we have no control over what happened to us, and sometimes we have to work through regret because of choices we made. Can you think of something in your life that you wish you could undo? How did you work through it?

12. Has there been an example of a person in your life who dealt with great loss in a positive way?

13. Julia told Gavin that he needed to forgive himself for what happened with his friend. Have you ever had to forgive yourself for a choice you made? Did you at first believe God wouldn't forgive you?

14. How was Julia able to take the horror of what happened to her and make something good come of it?

15. Julia learned never to take a normal life for granted. Can you list some of the ordinary things in your own life that you take for granted? Take a moment to thank God for each one of these blessings.

INSPIRATIONAL

Inspirational romances to warm your heart & soul.

SUSPENSE

TITLES AVAILABLE NEXT MONTH

Available August 9, 2011

AGENT UNDERCOVER
Rose Mountain Refuge
Lynette Eason

THE BABY'S BODYGUARD
Emerald Coast 911
Stephanie Newton

BURIED TRUTH
Dana Mentink

ON DEADLY GROUND
Lauren Nichols

LISCNM0711

REQUEST YOUR FREE BOOKS!
2 FREE RIVETING INSPIRATIONAL NOVELS
PLUS 2 FREE MYSTERY GIFTS

YES! Please send me 2 FREE Love Inspired® Suspense novels and my 2 FREE mystery gifts (gifts are worth about $10). After receiving them, if I don't wish to receive any more books, I can return the shipping statement marked "cancel". If I don't cancel, I will receive 4 brand-new novels every month and be billed just $4.49 per book in the U.S. or $4.99 per book in Canada. That's a saving of at least 22% off the cover price. It's quite a bargain! Shipping and handling is just 50¢ per book in the U.S. and 75¢ per book in Canada.* I understand that accepting the 2 free books and gifts places me under no obligation to buy anything. I can always return a shipment and cancel at any time. Even if I never buy another book, the two free books and gifts are mine to keep forever.

123/323 IDN FEHR

Name	(PLEASE PRINT)	
Address		Apt. #
City	State/Prov.	Zip/Postal Code

Signature (if under 18, a parent or guardian must sign)

Mail to the **Reader Service:**
IN U.S.A.: P.O. Box 1867, Buffalo, NY 14240-1867
IN CANADA: P.O. Box 609, Fort Erie, Ontario L2A 5X3

Not valid for current subscribers to Love Inspired Suspense books.

**Are you a subscriber to Love Inspired Suspense
and want to receive the larger-print edition?
Call 1-800-873-8635 or visit www.ReaderService.com.**

* Terms and prices subject to change without notice. Prices do not include applicable taxes. Sales tax applicable in N.Y. Canadian residents will be charged applicable taxes. Offer not valid in Quebec. This offer is limited to one order per household. All orders subject to credit approval. Credit or debit balances in a customer's account(s) may be offset by any other outstanding balance owed by or to the customer. Please allow 4 to 6 weeks for delivery. Offer available while quantities last.

Your Privacy—The Reader Service is committed to protecting your privacy. Our Privacy Policy is available online at www.ReaderService.com or upon request from the Reader Service.

We make a portion of our mailing list available to reputable third parties that offer products we believe may interest you. If you prefer that we not exchange your name with third parties, or if you wish to clarify or modify your communication preferences, please visit us at www.ReaderService.com/consumerchoice or write to us at Reader Service Preference Service, P.O. Box 9062, Buffalo, NY 14269. Include your complete name and address.

LISUS11B

DEA Agent Paige Ashworth's new assignment is to work undercover at a local elementary school to find out how her partner and his girlfriend died while trying to take down a drug ring. Read on for a sneak preview of AGENT UNDERCOVER by Lynette Eason, available August 2011 only from Love Inspired Suspense.

Pain. That was Paige's first thought. Her first feeling. Her first piece of awareness.

It felt like shards of glass bit into her skull with relentless determination. Her eyes fluttered and she thought she saw someone seated in the chair next to her.

Why was she in bed?

Memories flitted back. Bits and pieces. A little boy. A school. A crosswalk. A speeding car.

And she'd pedaled like a madwoman to dart in front of the car to rescue the child.

A gasp escaped her and she woke a little more. The pain faded to a dull throb. Where was the little boy? Was he all right?

Warmth covered her left hand. Someone held it. Who?

Awareness struggled into full consciousness, and she opened her eyes to stare into one of the most beautiful faces she'd ever seen. Aquamarine eyes crinkled at the corners and full lips curved into a smile.

The lips spoke. "Hello, welcome back."

Another sweet face pushed its way into her line of sight. A little boy about six years old.

"Hi," she whispered.

The hand over hers squeezed. "You saved Will's life, you know."

She had? Will. The little boy had a name. "Oh. Good."

Her smiled slipped into a frown. "I was afraid I couldn't do it. That car…"

"I'm Dylan Seabrook. This is my nephew, Will Price."

The name jolted her. Doing her best to keep her expression neutral, she simply smiled at him. She wanted to nod, but didn't dare.

Closing her eyes, Paige could see the racing car coming closer, hear the roar of the engine…

She flicked her eyelids up. "Did they catch him? Whoever was in the car?"

Dylan shook his head. "No. He—or she—never stopped."

She sighed. "Well, I'm glad Will is okay. That's all that really matters." Well, that, and whether or not she'd just blown her cover to save this child—the son of the woman whose death she was supposed to be investigating.

For more, pick up AGENT UNDERCOVER
by Lynette Eason, available August 2011
from Love Inspired Suspense.

Fighting to earn respect as the new town marshal, Danna Carpenter teams up with detective Chas O'Grady for help. But when circumstances place them in a compromising situation, the town forces a more permanent partnership—marriage. If they can let down their guards with each other they might find that love is the greatest catch of all.

Marrying Miss Marshal
by
LACY WILLIAMS

Available August wherever books are sold.

www.LoveInspiredBooks.com